Horrendous Habits

Philip Ardagh gets to write this blurb himself so it probably contains a pack of lies. A pack of lies is usually made up of fifty-two cards and, more often than not, two jokers. This blurb also contains a free set of steak knives for one lucky reader. Sadly, that's not you.

FICTION

The Eddie Dickens Trilogy
Awful End
Dreadful Acts
Terrible Times

The Further Adventures of Eddie Dickens
Dubious Deeds

Unlikely Exploits
The Fall of Fergal
Heir of Mystery
The Rise of the House of McNally

NON-FICTION

The Hieroglyphs Handbook
Teach Yourself Ancient Egyptian

The Archaeologist's Handbook
The Insider's Guide to Digging up the Past

Did Dinosaurs Snore?
100½ Questions about Dinosaurs Answered

Why Are Castles Castle-Shaped?
100½ Questions about Castles Answered

FOR ADULTS

The Not-So-Very-Nice Goings-On at Victoria Lodge
Without Illustrations by the Author

PHILIP ARDAGH

HORRENDOUS HABITS

Book Two of
The Further Adventures of Eddie Dickens

illustrated by David Roberts

ff

faber and faber

For my son, Frederick.
Hi, Freddie!

First published in 2005
by Faber and Faber Limited
3 Queen Square, London WC1N 3AU

Typeset by Faber and Faber Limited
Printed in England by Mackays of Chatham plc, Chatham, Kent

© Philip Ardagh, 2005
Illustrations © David Roberts, 2005

Philip Ardagh is hereby identified as author of this work in accordance
with Section 77 of the Copyright, Designs and Patents Act 1988

A CIP record for this book
is available from the British Library

ISBN 0-571–21709–5

2 4 6 8 10 9 7 5 3 1

A Message from the Author

Who's admiring his new pair of trousers

This book is full of monks. In fact, it's *so* full of monks that my wife Héloïse suggested that I call it 'Monkey Business' but, as you can see, I didn't. It's a very good title though, but please don't tell her I said so. I don't want to encourage her. Where would it end?

In the previous Further Adventure, *Dubious Deeds*, Eddie spent most of his time in Scotland. This time around he's much closer to home but might just as well be in Scotland because he can't remember where he lives.

Confused? Then read on . . .

PHILIP ARDAGH
East Sussex
2005

Contents

A New Arrival

*In which, somewhat surprisingly,
a baby is found in the bulrushes*

'What is it?' demanded Even Madder Aunt Maud, stomping towards a patch of bulrushes, with Malcolm her stuffed stoat (who looked suspiciously like a stuffed ferret) under one arm.

'It sounds like a baby,' said Eddie, above the wailing which had attracted them down to the water's edge in the first place. (At Even Madder Aunt Maud's insistence, she and Eddie had been playing an unusual game of croquet on the lower lawn at Awful End. Unusual because, instead of

1

croquet balls, they'd been using croquet turnips, or 'rutabagas' as our American friends would say. She'd found a whole sack of them down by the compost heaps and hadn't wanted them to go to waste.)

Eddie ran past Maud to the edge of the ornamental lake. 'Yes!' he cried. 'It's a baby!'

'A baby what?' demanded Even Madder Aunt Maud.

'A baby,' Eddie repeated, wading into the shallows and parting the bulrushes. He didn't think he could put it any more simply than that.

'A baby carrot? A baby carriage? A baby possum?' Even Madder Aunt Maud wanted to know. She'd recently read about the extraordinary wildlife of the continent of Australia in a book entitled *The Extraordinary Wildlife of the Continent of Australia* and was delighted to have the opportunity to introduce the word possum into a conversation quite legitimately. (It's a tree-dwelling animal with a pouch like a kangaroo's and a tail designed for grasping branches, in case you didn't already know.)

'A baby *baby*,' said Eddie, lifting the crying child out of a basket firmly wedged amongst the tall stalks at the water's edge. (That's the tall stalks of the bulrushes, of course, spelled s-t-a-l-k-s. I don't want you to go thinking that the baby in the basket was in the lake wedged between the bird kind of storks, spelled s-t-o-r-k-s. It's important to clear this up right now because, in Eddie's day, children were often told that it was the stork – the bird not the bulrush stems – that delivered new babies to households.) 'It's a human baby.'

Eddie held the crying infant in his arms and waded back on to the lawn. It stopped crying almost immediately.

Even Madder Aunt Maud glared down at the little bundle of joy. 'It's got a very large head,' she announced.

'Babies generally have, Mad Aunt Maud,' said Eddie.

'What was it doing floating around in my lake like . . . like . . .'

'Like Moses in the bulrushes?' Eddie suggested helpfully.

'Who in the what?' asked his great-aunt.

'Moses in the Bible,' said Eddie.

'I thought you said in the bulrushes?' said Even Madder Aunt Maud, narrowing her eyes as though suspecting Eddie of playing some trick on her.

'Moses in the bulrushes in the Bible,' he explained.

Even Madder Aunt Maud seemed to have absolutely no idea what he was talking about, so she hit him over the head with Malcolm. 'Oh do be quiet,' she said.

3

The moment the very rigid (and very hard) stuffed stoat came into contact with Eddie's head, it was the babe in his arms who cried out and not Eddie. It glared at Even Madder Aunt Maud and let out a particularly plaintive wail.

'That thing just threatened me!' said EMAM in amazement. 'Did you see the look it gave me? Well, did you?'

'It's only a baby, Mad Aunt Maud,' said Eddie. 'I'm sure it meant no harm.'

'Then what was it doing lurking in my cake?'

'You mean lake,' Eddie corrected her, as politely as possible.

'And she said lake,' said Eddie's father, Mr Dickens, appearing at her side. 'The cake thing was a typing error. Mr Ardagh gets sloppy like that sometimes. Some readers even write in to complain.'

Eddie had less than no idea of what his father was talking about.

'Where did you find that child?' Mr Dickens wanted to know.

'It was in a basket in the bulrushes,' said Eddie.

'Like Moses in the Bible,' said Even Madder Aunt Maud, which surprised Eddie more than a little.

'What kind of basket?' asked Mr Dickens.

'Does that matter, Father?' asked Eddie. 'I

mean, shouldn't we get the poor thing inside and make sure it's dry and . . . and suchlike?'

'Matter? Of course it matters. If we are to return this baby to its rightful owners, then the basket might contain a vital clue as to their identity.'

Even Madder Aunt Maud was seized by the idea and when she was seized by an idea she ran with it, mixed metaphors or no mixed metaphors. 'If it's a laundry basket, then the baby's parents could work in a laundry. If it's a snake charmer's basket, its parents could be snake charmers. If it's a picnic basket, its parents could . . . could, er –'

'Like sandwiches?' Mr Dickens suggested, helpfully, one eyebrow – though I'm not sure which – slightly raised.

Eddie carefully handed the baby, who was wrapped in a snow-white blanket, to his father, who accepted him – he'll turn out to be a he – like a man who'd never held a baby in his life. He'd certainly never held Eddie when he was a baby. Victorian fathers didn't generally do such things. Their job as fathers was to look at their offspring over the top of a newspaper once in a while, or demand to see them in their study in their Sunday best.

The baby now safely in Mr Dickens's arms (where he started wailing again the moment Eddie let go of him), Eddie waded back into the shallows of the ornamental lake and dragged out the basket.

He inspected it. It was a very ordinary basketylooking basket and there was no conveniently placed luggage label with a name and address on it, either. In fact, there was no label of any kind, and nothing to offer any obvious clues that Eddie could see. 'It's just a basket,' he said.

'Couldn't we put it back?' suggested Even Madder Aunt Maud, looking down at the baby.

'WAAAAAAAAAAAAAAAAAA!' said the baby (for much longer than space in this book permits).

'The basket or the baby, Even Madder Aunt Maud?' asked a disbelieving Eddie.

'Put it back?' asked Mr Dickens above the din, raising the other eyebrow (whichever one that was). He handed his son the baby, who instantly fell silent again.

'In my youth, I went fishing with my brothers

in the lochs of Scotland,' said Even Madder Aunt Maud. 'If they didn't like the look of a fish they caught, they put it back.'

'Hmmm,' said Mr Dickens. 'An interesting idea, aunt,' he said, 'but might I suggest that it's rather a short term solution.'

'But you never had any brothers,' Eddie pointed out as politely as possible.

'And we never went fishing!' Even Madder Aunt Maud added triumphantly, as though this were some sort of game and she'd just scored big points off Eddie.

'I'll take the baby to mother. She'll know what to do,' said Eddie, though the truth be told, he rather suspected that she might not. In the brief time that Eddie had not been at school or at sea in his early childhood, Eddie had been looked after by Nanny Louche, an onion-seller by profession who'd been given the job of caring for Baby Edmund by default. (Here, 'by default' means 'by mistake', only more so.) Eddie had no memory of her now, but had a nice warm feeling every time he smelt raw unpeeled onions or saw someone wearing a stripy shirt.

He eventually found his mother in the drawing-room, unravelling the flowery-patterned cover of one of the armchairs. 'This will make useful string,' she explained, rolling the unpicked thread into a ball. 'Is that your baby, dearest?'

'No, Mother. I just found it.'

'Well you can't keep it, I'm afraid, Edmund. They're very demanding and very expensive to maintain. I had one once, you know.'

'Yes I do know, Mother,' said Eddie. 'That was me.'

Mrs Dickens got up off her knees and sat herself down in the chair that she'd been quietly ruining. 'Why so it was!' she laughed. 'Now do explain what's going on.'

Eddie sat on a footstool opposite her, still carefully cradling the baby in his arms. The baby gurgled contentedly, whilst the water in Eddie's shoes squelched noisily. He'd left a trail of muddy wet footprints across the room. 'Even Madder Aunt Maud and I were playing croquet on the lower lawn when we heard a baby crying and I found it in a basket in the bulrushes, like Moses.'

'Like who, dear?'

'Moses –' said Eddie.

'Moses?'

'Never mind, Mother,' said Eddie. 'I was wondering what we should do with it.'

'Do?' asked his mother.

'With the baby,' said Eddie. 'To make sure that it's comfortable and unharmed.'

Mrs Dickens leant forward and unwrapped the

8

blanket. 'It,' she pronounced, 'is a he, and he looks perfectly happy to me. If he were hungry, unhappy or in pain he'd be crying.'

'That's a relief, mother,' said Eddie, wrapping him up again. 'Shouldn't you take him?'

'Where?'

'Out of my arms.'

'Why?'

That was a good question. 'Because – er – you're a grown-up and a mother and you understand these things.'

Mrs Dickens laughed again. 'Really, Edmund! Where do you get such ideas from? Just because I'm an adult and a mother doesn't mean I can make the slightest sense of this world, or anyone in it!'

'Then what shall I do with him?' asked Eddie, looking down at the baby, who looked back up at him with a pair of big, trusting, clear-blue eyes.

'Name him, of course,' said Eddie's mother. 'You can't go around calling him "it" or "him" all the time.'

Eddie stood up and walked over to one of the huge windows overlooking the lawn, sloping down to the lake in the distance.

'But what about his parents?' said Eddie.

'They can call him what they like,' said Mrs Dickens.

'Shouldn't we try to find them?'

'Perhaps your father could place an advertisement in the local newspaper,' she suggested. '"Found, one baby boy." They're bound to notice he's missing sooner or later.'

'But what if it was his mother or father who put him in the basket in the first place?' Eddie suggested. 'Maybe they couldn't afford to look after him –'

'It's an expensive blanket,' Mrs Dickens commented. She had joined her son by the window and was picking at the corner of the material.

'So it is!' said Eddie, clearly impressed. 'I think I shall call him Ned.' Eddie had recently been reading about the remarkable exploits of Ned Kelly, the Australian outlaw, in a book entitled *The Remarkable Exploits of Ned Kelly, The Australian Outlaw*, and thought the name rather exciting. (In case you were wondering, an Australian cousin on Eddie's mother's side of the family had recently

10

sent over a whole box of books. I've no idea why.)

'Baby Ned,' said Mrs Dickens. 'An excellent choice, Eddie.'

Much to Eddie's amazement, it was Gibbering Jane who took charge of Baby Ned. All Eddie had ever heard her do was gibber – hence the name – but the first thing she said on seeing the baby was, 'Oh, ain't he cute, Master Edmund? Can I 'old 'im?' and, when he passed Ned over, Eddie was delighted to find that the baby didn't start bawling again. It turned out that Jane (a failed chambermaid who spent most of her time in a cupboard under the stairs but, nowadays, did a few light duties about the place too) had been the second eldest of twelve children and had helped to bring up some of the younger ones before she'd ended up in service (which, in her case, meant working for the Dickenses).

In next to no time, she'd found some old napkins to use as nappies and had washed and changed Ned. She took the cutlery drawer out of an empty old kitchen dresser in one of the many unused rooms in the house, and turned it into a cot for him.

'What about food?' asked Eddie. 'What do babies eat?'

'Don't you worry about that,' said Jane.

Eddie was incredibly impressed. He left Ned

11

cooing happily, and went in search of his father, squelching his way around the house and garden.

Unfortunately, he found Mr Dickens in conversation with Mad Uncle Jack at the foot of his tree house (in which his great-uncle now lived much of the time). Unfortunately because Eddie knew that, with MUJ around, a straightforward conversation would be out of the question.

'I was wondering how we should go about locating the baby's parents, Father,' said Eddie tentatively.

'What kind of tree am I?' barked Mad Uncle Jack, no pun intended. Tree . . . bark . . . Never mind.

'I'm sorry?' asked Eddie.

'I should have thought that the question was perfectly clear,' said Mad Uncle Jack.

'I – er –'

'Do I speak with a stutter?'

'No –'

'Was I whispering?'

'No, I –'

'Was I speaking Chinese?'

'It's not that, Mad Unc–'

'Then what kind of tree am I?'

'It's a puzzle, my boy,' said Mr Dickens. 'Your great-uncle is asking you a riddle.'

'Oh, I see,' said Eddie, somewhat relieved. 'I don't know, Mad Uncle Jack. What kind of tree are you?'

'Tree?'

'Yes. I give up,' said Eddie. 'What kind of tree are you?'

'TREE?'

'Yes,' said Eddie, a little nervously now. 'W-What kind of tree are you?'

Mad Uncle Jack glared at him and frowned one of his thinnest of thin frowns above his thinnest of thin noses. 'Tree? Don't be so damned impertinent!'

Seeing his son's predicament, Mr Dickens came to Eddie's rescue. 'We'll see if anyone comes to the house asking about the missing child,' he said, 'and, if not, we'll inform the authorities.'

'Good idea,' said Eddie. They had a plan at last.

'I'm an oak!' laughed Mad Uncle Jack. He now had an acorn hanging from either ear, like a pair of nature's ear-rings.

Episode 2

Disaster Strikes

*In which we learn of a proposed beating,
and end with a 'CRUNCH!'*

The following morning, Eddie didn't get to see Baby Ned before breakfast, which began with his father announcing that – No, hang on, let him tell it:

'Today is the annual beating the bounds!' said Mr Dickens over the top of the bacon piled high on his plate.

'What's that, Father?' asked Eddie politely.

'Questions! Questions!' said his father.

'It means once-a-year,' said his mother from her end of the table.

'I know what annual means, Mother,' said Eddie. 'I was wondering about the beating the bounds part.'

14

'Questions! Questions!' his father repeated.

Eddie reached for the china marmalade pot. It was shaped like an orange, with the leaves on the top acting as the handle to the lid. He lifted it. The pot was empty.

'We appear to have run out of marmalade,' said Eddie.

'Disgraceful!' said Mr Dickens. 'Ring for Daphne.'

Dawkins was Mr Dickens's gentleman's gentleman but, since coming with them to Awful End, now did just about everything around the house . . . but Mr Dickens called him Daphne. He wasn't good at remembering names.

Eddie got up from his seat and yanked the bell pull. Down in the depths of Awful End, a little bell (in a row of little bells) rang. Dawkins looked up from the ironing-board on which he was ironing his favourite pieces of tissue paper and, by looking at the label under the jangling bell, which read 'Morning Room', he could see where his services were required. He put down the iron, slipped on the jacket of his suit and began the long trek up the stairs.

Meanwhile, Mr Dickens was explaining 'beating the bounds' to his son.

'The age-old tradition of beating the bounds goes back hundreds of years in this country,

Jonathan.' (See? I told you he was bad with names.) 'Its origins have been lost in the mists of time.'

'Oranges?' asked Mrs Dickens. 'Did you say oranges, dear?'

'Origins,' repeated Mr Dickens.

'I'm sorry,' said his wife. 'I was sure you said oranges.'

Mr Dickens chewed on a piece of bacon and gave his wife a funny look. She didn't seem to know what to do with it, so she gave it straight back. Watching the funny look pass between them – quite a feat when they were at opposite ends of an impressively long breakfast table – Eddie wished his father would hurry up and explain the bounds part and get on to the beating. It sounded painful.

'The bounds in question are boundaries, so if, for example, you're beating the parish bounds it would be the perimeter of the parish.' Mr Dickens pulled a small piece of bacon rind from his mouth, which had been lodged between his teeth.

At that moment, Dawkins entered the breakfast room. He was about to say one of his favourite lines, 'You rang, sir?' (which is one of the first things they teach you to say at gentleman's gentleman school), when Eddie's mother pre-empted him, which isn't as painful as it sounds. It simply means 'got in there before he did'.

'Oranges,' she said. 'We've run out of oranges.'

'Origins, not oranges,' Mr Dickens corrected her.

'Marmalade,' Eddie corrected them both. 'Could we have some more marmalade, please, Dawkins?'

'Very good, Master Edmund,' said Dawkins, taking the empty pot in his gloved hand and leaving the room. (That 'very good' wasn't a 'very good' as in 'well done' but as in 'yes, I'll do that at once'.)

'Where was I?' asked Mr Dickens. 'I suspect these interruptions add nothing to the plot.'

'You were about to explain the beating part,' his son reminded him.

'Tradition has it that, once a year, people would walk along a boundary, beating the ground with sticks,' Mr Dickens continued. 'This would have two functions: firstly, in order to remind everyone who traipsed after the beater exactly where the boundary was and, secondly, to thrash aside any

17

nettles – for example – which may be obscuring the boundary.'

Mrs Dickens laughed.

'What's funny about that, my love?' asked her husband.

'I wasn't laughing at your explanation,' Eddie's mother explained. 'It's simply that I've made an amusing face out of the food upon my breakfast plate.'

She held up the plate and turned it around for them to see. The sausage nose, rasher-of-bacon mouth and mushroom eyes did, indeed, make an impressive face. The scrambled-egg hair was a stroke of genius. What was equally impressive was the way in which she'd managed to stick everything in place so that it hadn't slid off the plate when she held it up at right angles to the table. She'd used marmalade. Hence the empty pot.

'Enchanting,' said Mr Dickens. He loved most things about his wife, including the way she played with her food. They'd first met as children and, during one of their earliest encounters, she'd been in the middle of a game of hide-and-seek with a bowl of trifle.

She put her plate back down on the linen tablecloth, and Eddie's father went on with his explanation. 'An alternative version of beating the bounds has a boy being beaten at regular intervals

18

along the boundary. If you do this, he isn't going to forget the route in a hurry, now, is he?'

The door opened and Dawkins re-entered the room, the refilled orange-shaped marmalade pot on a silver salver (which is a small round tray). He placed it in front of Eddie. 'Your marmalade, Master Edmund,' he said.

'Thank you very much,' said Eddie.

The gentleman's gentleman nodded and left the room, eager to get back to ironing his tissue paper. He loved tissue paper and his favourite tissue paper was freshly-ironed tissue paper, still warm.

Whilst Eddie spread the marmalade on his toast (from which he'd already pulled the watch springs his mother insisted on being added to the flour), and whilst his mother proceeded to pull each item of food off her plate with her fingers, lick the marmalade glue from the back and put it back down again, Mr Dickens proceeded to explain the Awful End approach to beating the bounds.

'It isn't common practice for private estates to have beating the bounds ceremonies, but Mad Uncle Jack says that it's been going on here for as long as he can remember.'

'But if it's an annual event, Father, why haven't I seen it before?' asked Eddie, which was a good question. Eddie and his parents had been living at Awful End for a few years by then.

His father was about to say 'Questions! Questions!' yet *again*, when Mad Uncle Jack burst through the door in person. (Mad Uncle Jack was the person, not the door.)

'Good morning, everybody!' he said, his eyes twinkling with excitement above his beakiest of beaky noses. 'Today's the day!'

'No one could argue with that, Mudge!' said Mrs Dickens, 'mudge' being how one pronounces MUJ unless one says 'em-ew-jay.'

'I want everyone up and out of here and ready to witness the beating of the bounds by ten o'clock,' announced Eddie's great-uncle.

'What about Baby Ned –?' Eddie began.

'We've fine weather for it!' said MUJ. He spun around one-hundred-and-eighty degrees and strode out of the room as fast as his spindly legs would allow.

At that precise moment a horrible thought struck Eddie. The colour drained from his face. (There's no point in looking for the nearest illustration. They're all in black and white.) His father said that, traditionally, it was a *boy* who was beaten when beating the bounds: a b-o-y.

The last time that he'd checked, he was the only boy at Awful End, apart from Ned, of course, who was more of a baby than a boy. In a *typical* house of that size there would have been numerous servants including, at the very least, a boot boy, but Awful End was far from typical. The house itself was occupied by Eddie and his parents, Dawkins and Gibbering Jane. Mad Uncle Jack lived in the tree house in the grounds; Even Madder Aunt Maud lived in Marjorie (a giant hollow cow) in the rose garden; and then there was the handful of ex-soldiers on the estate, who'd once served under Mad Uncle Jack in his regiment.

Fortunately for Eddie, it transpired that Mad Uncle Jack and Even Madder Aunt Maud had a slightly different approach to the more traditional beating the bounds. Each year – on the years that they remembered to do it, that is (and no one was in a hurry to remind them) – they now beat one of the ex-soldiers with Maud's stuffed stoat Malcolm (or was it Sally?).

Each year, MUJ asked for a volunteer from their ranks and each year one of their number was pushed forward by the others to act as the unwilling participant.

In the year that the events in this Further Adventures unfolded, Mad Uncle Jack's ex-soldiers were spending much of their time working on the vast cast-iron bridge he was having constructed between his tree house and Marjorie the hollow cow ('So that I can hurry to my love pumpkin with grace and ease' was how he'd put it. The love pumpkin, of course, being his dear wife Even Madder Aunt Maud).

The bridge was designed by that fairly well-known engineer Fandango Jones who – according to him, at least – had once worked alongside the very famous Victorian engineer Isambard Kingdom Brunel. What no one ever dared ask, and Fandango Jones never volunteered, was what kind of work it was, exactly, that he'd done alongside Brunel. Some of the less kind critics of his work have suggested that it was carrying the great man's hat, others that it was selling those little bags of roast chestnuts, but we can't be sure. What we *can* be sure about, though, was that Isambard Kingdom Brunel was a better engineer than Fandango Jones, which is probably why he had three names when Fandango Jones only had two.

According to an anonymous pamphlet praising the life and achievement of Fandango Jones, published a year or so before his death (and probably by Jones himself, with help with the spelling of some of the harder words from his wife Clarissa), Jones's given name was Clement; it being a tradition in his branch of the Jones family that all eldest sons were called 'Clement'. On page three of *Bridging the Gap: Being the Life of that Fairly Well-Known Engineer Fandango Jones*, it reveals that this Clement Jones gained the nickname Fandango from the way in which he would explain his latest design by 'pacing it out upon the floor, with the sure and swift-footedness of one dancing the fandango' but, I assume, without the aid of castanets or a tambourine.

As well as being a little – how shall I put it? – eccentric, Mr Jones was also quite frightening to look at. He was small and squat with a stovepipe hat – made from two stovepipe hats riveted together to give it extra height – and very bushy side-whiskers which his loving wife Clarissa referred to as his 'mutton chops'. What was most unusual, though, was that the small round spectacles he wore at all times contained blue tinted lenses. Most unfortunate (and this is well recorded, but not in the pamphlet *Bridging the Gap: Being the Life of that Fairly Well-Known Engineer Fandango Jones*) is the fact that he was one of those people who spat when he spoke . . .

. . . which is why, when Eddie and his parents congregated at the front of the house after a marmalade-filled breakfast, Eddie found Even Madder Aunt Maud had her umbrella up and in front of her whilst in conversation with the engineer.

'But why iron?' she was arguing for the umpteenth time. 'Why not wood? A wooden bridge would do.'

'Your husband specifically specified an iron bridge, madam,' said Fandango Jones, spraying EMAM's umbrella as he spoke.

'Or rope? I believe in some parts of the empire, there are some perfectly good rope bridges.'

'The use of iron was at your husband's insistence.'

'Or paper. I have it on good authority that the Japanese build the walls of their houses from paper. How about a nice paper bridge? *Thick* paper mind you.'

'Madam. The choice of material was not mine, but –'

'Or soup. Why not a bridge of soup?'

'Soup?'

'Soup!'

'That's –' Fandango Jones was about to say 'madness' when he stopped himself. Not because he thought it'd be rude to call his current employer's wife mad – with a name such as Even Madder Mrs Dickens it might even be considered appropriate – but because the thought occurred to him that this lady brandishing a stuffed stoat in one hand and an umbrella in the other might have a point. If no one had built a bridge of soup before, and he was to do so, then he could be the first! He could imagine the headline in *Civil Engineers Bi-Monthly*: **'FANDANGO JONES BUILDS FIRST BRIDGE MADE FROM SOUP'**. It was when he was imagining the subheading: **'They Said It Could Not Be Done'**, that his face fell. Of course it couldn't be done. It was an impossible idea. It was a ridiculous, silly idea. 'The bridge is to be made of iron, madam, and there's an end to it.'

It was just as Jones spat out the word 'it' that a chimney (shaped like a giant barley sugar, apparently) fell from the roof of Awful End and landed on Eddie's father, Mr Dickens, with a fairly dreadful 'CRUNCH'.

Episode 3

Flat Out

In which fate, in the form of a chimney,
deals a blow to poor Mr Dickens

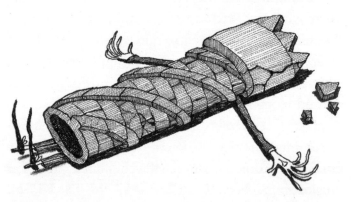

I once wrote a book called *Heir of Mystery* and in it is a picture of a man, named Vern De Vere, lying under a large sign that fell off the wall of an army recruiting office and landed on top of him. You couldn't tell that it was Mr De Vere because all that was sticking out from under the sign were his arms and legs.

As you can see, this would have been very similar to the sight that faced Mr Dickens's relatives as they looked down on the poor man trapped under the chimney stack.

Unlike Mr De Vere, who didn't survive his tragic accident, Mr Dickens was alive and, if not exactly well, at least groaning. Mrs Dickens thought she heard her husband mutter 'I'll get you for this, Ardagh!' but put it down to the ramblings of a seriously injured man. It made no sense at all.

It was Eddie who suggested that they lift the large chunk of stone off his father. The others were busy gawping. With the help of Ex-Private Drabb (who'd been 'volunteered' to be beaten in that year's beating the bounds), Eddie lifted up the chimney and dropped it to one side. It made quite a thud when it hit the driveway.

Ex-Private Drabb looked surprisingly muscular for a man of his age, for he was, to borrow my mother's phrase, 'no spring chicken'. This was misleading. Those weren't really broad shoulders, a large chest and muscles bulging under his clothing; he had various cushions stuffed in there to act as padding. Padding against what? Being beaten with a stuffed stoat at regular intervals, that's what.

I think there's a saying along the lines of 'one man's misfortune is another man's fortune' and if there isn't there should be. Poor old Mr Dickens being flattened by one of Awful End's numerous chimneys may have been rather bad luck for Mr Dickens, but was excellent news for Ex-Private Drabb. Beating the bounds of the Awful End estate would be postponed or, if luck was *really* on his side, maybe even cancelled altogether.

The chimney removed, Mrs Dickens threw herself to the gravelly ground and cradled her husband in her marmalade-stained lap. 'Speak to me!' she pleaded.

'Father!' Eddie cried. 'Are you all right?'

'Damn and confound it!' said Mad Uncle Jack, looking up at the roof. 'More repairs!'

'Get up, lazy-bones,' said Even Madder Aunt Maud prodding Mr Dickens with the tip of her now-closed umbrella (which made a change from using the tip of Malcolm's nose).

'Father!' Eddie repeated.

'Why can't I be in a book about nice fluffy bunnies where not much happens?' groaned Mr Dickens.

'Mad!' said Even Madder Aunt Maud. 'He's gone quite mad. We'll have to have him shot.'

'*Fwumbblewww*,' said Mrs Dickens, who'd now filled her mouth with gravel to calm her nerves.

'I'll fetch Dawkins,' said Ex-Private Drabb, scuttling off into the house.

'Roof tiles are expensive enough,' muttered MUJ, 'but a whole replacement chimney?'

'Hmmmm,' said Fandango Jones, who'd produced a notebook from his pocket and was writing notes and drawing angles and lines and diagrams with a stubby pencil. 'Most interesting.'

'We must get a stonemason!' said Mad Uncle Jack.

'We must get sandwiches!' said Even Madder Aunt Maud.

'We must get the police!' spat Mr Jones, the engineer, having completed some complicated calculations in his head.

'We must get a DOCTOR!' shouted Eddie.

That shut them all up.

'Yes,' said Mad Uncle Jack, looking down at Eddie's father as though he'd forgotten he was lying there. 'We must send Dawkins to fetch Doctor Humple at once.'

'And have him bring sandwiches!' Even Madder Aunt Maud added. 'And what fillings would my little Malcolm like?' she asked the stuffed stoat. It said nothing, giving her a glassy stare. No surprises there, then.

Nowadays we know that we shouldn't move people when they've been injured, until the professionals arrive. Back in those days, it was thought that you'd be better off lying on a bed or a couch or something more comfortable than a gravel driveway if you'd just been hit by a chimney. In fact, in *Old Roxbee's Book of Common Household Ailments*, under 'Injuries Incurred Upon Being Hit By A Fallen Chimney' it states:

29

In order to assist the poor unfortunate struck by said chimney, remove him to a comfortable spot and tenderly apply a bread poultice to the affected area, offering gentle words of encouragement throughout the treatment. If the patient's life appears to be in serious danger, do not feel it your duty to inform him, but simply offer a soothing, 'There, there,' whilst patting his hand with your own.

The advice, of course, applied equally well to 'shes' as 'hes', but it was usually only men who got a mention in such books of the time, except in sections particularly devoted to women, dealing with such matters as 'Upon Being Upset by a Fellow Guest at a Ladies' Luncheon Party', 'Upon Having An Attack of the Vapours' and 'Upon Being Confronted by a Particularly Unpleasant Shade of Pink Without Sufficient Warning'.

Fortunately for Eddie's father, there wasn't a copy of *Old Roxbee's Book of Common Household Ailments* to be found in Awful End, or he'd probably have suffered more pain and indignity than being carried to a *chaise longue* in the withdrawing room, which would, no doubt, have involved covering him from head to toe – because his 'affected area' was just about everywhere – in porridge, it being the closest thing to a poultice they'd have to hand. Having said that, as you'll discover, the Dickenses had their own ideas.

It was whilst Dawkins and Ex-Private Drabb were doing the carrying that there was a nasty clicking sound and Dawkins's back locked in position. His back locking in position meant that Dawkins could no longer stand up straight and certainly was in no position to ride a horse into town to fetch Dr Humple. Which is how Eddie came to volunteer to take the pony and trap . . . and, dear reader, how he came to have a terrible accident of his own.

The pony which was pulling the trap (more than a cart but less than a carriage) that Eddie was sitting in hadn't belonged to the Dickens family for very long. His name was Horsey and he'd been given to Eddie's father by the Thackerys who'd been their nearest neighbours when they'd lived in their previous house (since burnt to the ground). The Thackerys – not to be confused with the Thackerays, of whom the famous author William Makepeace Thackeray was one – were fairly regular visitors to Awful End, though they did their best to stay out of the way of Mad Uncle Jack and Even Madder Aunt Maud. It was Laudanum and Florinda they'd come to see. ('Mr and Mrs Dickens' to you and me. Or 'mother and father' to

Eddie.) Hey! Wait a minute. I think this is the very first time in five books that I've actually told you Eddie's parents' first names. I hope it was worth the wait.

Jonas Thackery and his wife Emily had eight children, the youngest (Joy) being just a few years old and the oldest (Thomas) being older than his mother, for legal reasons. (It had something to do with inheritance and taxes.) The Thackerys loved animals and the children were forever looking after birds with broken wings or rabbits with a slight limp, even if it meant injuring them in the first place.

They were never more happy than when they were nursing a pig back to health or informing a goat that her kid would make a full recovery. They'd gained quite a reputation locally when Mrs Thackery had managed to nurse an injured racehorse named *Forward Motion* (in italics) back to health when the usual prescription was shooting them. The cure had involved the use of a great deal of something called 'rubbing alcohol' and a variety of different herbs. Mrs Thackery was drunk for weeks and her breath stank of ragwort, but the horse made a full recovery.

At the very first race *Forward Motion* (in italics) ran in after his miraculous cure, he was so full of energy that he galloped straight into the stands and trampled several race-goers to death. Fortunately for the Thackerys, the race-goers were from abroad and, not being British, the tragedy didn't merit more than a few lines in the national newspapers.

The only Thackery who didn't like animals one tiny bit (except on his plate with at least two vegetables) was David Thackery, who was about Eddie's age. When he grew up, he wanted to be a man of the cloth. Despite what it may sound like, 'a man of the cloth' isn't a window cleaner or even a tailor but another name for a churchman. His ultimate aim was to be an archbishop (or, perhaps, a saint), but he'd be happy starting off as a rector or a vicar or something like that.

David Thackery was always quick to point out that animals didn't have souls and couldn't go to heaven, so wouldn't his parents and siblings be better off caring for less fortunate people rather than wasting their time with silly-old-animals? This would usually cause his mother to burst into tears and to bury her face in the nearest furry patient.

Whenever Mr and Mrs Thackery came to visit the Dickens at Awful End, they always brought one or other of their children with them and at least one animal. On the occasion that they'd brought Horsey as a present, they'd also brought David. Whilst Laudanum and Florinda Dickens and Jonas and Emily Thackery went inside for tea, Eddie and David were instructed to 'take the air'. (They didn't have to take it anywhere except inside their lungs. It was a way of telling them to go outside.)

'Show Edmund what we've brought the family this time, dearest,' Mrs Thackery had instructed her son.

Eddie had been delighted with Horsey, but time spent with David was always a different matter. And now Eddie and Horsey were heading for Dr Humple, and that terrible, terrible accident I already mentioned. The suspense is killing me.

A Crash after the Crunch

*In which Eddie Dickens
doesn't know he is*

Eddie's biggest problem at that precise moment was that he didn't know that he was. Eddie Dickens, that is. All he knew for sure was that he was lying face-down in a gorse bush and that his head hurt. Quite a lot of him hurt, in fact. Gorse bushes are renowned for their prickles and a good percentage of prickles from this particular bush were sticking into him. Now Eddie knew what it would feel like to be a hedgehog who'd absent-mindedly put his coat on inside out.

Eddie managed to struggle free of the bush, tearing much of his clothing, and some of his skin, in the process. Upright and dizzy, he looked around. 'Who am I?' he wondered, and only then did he wonder *where* he was.

Eddie's left knee hurt even more than his head and he found it difficult to scramble up the grassy bank to the road but, whoever he might turn out to be, he knew that he couldn't lie around in a gorse bush in a ditch all day.

Eddie didn't know what to expect as he climbed the bank but, one thing's for certain, it wasn't a bright red dragon carrying a basket of fruit. But that's exactly what he did see.

The dragon smiled. 'Apple?' it asked, though I somehow wish it had said 'banana'.

Eddie collapsed to the ground unconscious.

Time passed. Eddie opened his eyes. He was staring up at a ceiling; and what a ceiling.

Where on Earth was he? Lying in the middle of a cathedral or something? How had he got there? He tried to sit up. His head swam. He felt all woo-oo-oo-oozy and he was disoriented, which means the same as 'disorientated' but is shorter.

'*Wozzgowinnon?*' he slurred.

He felt a hand on his shoulder. 'Rest, my child,' said a kindly voice.

'*Hooamma? Wurramma?*' he asked, which may sound a bit like the way some of the Scottish folk spoke in the first book in these Further Adventures, but actually meant 'Who am I? Where am I?', which were both perfectly reasonable questions under the circumstances.

'Rest now, questions later,' said the man – yes it was definitely a man – with the kindly voice.

Eddie looked at him. The man was no oil-painting. He looked quite frightening, in fact; his face half in shadow beneath some kind of hood. He looked sinister. He had a very, *very* large nose which was very, *very* warty, and he had three peg-like teeth overhanging his lower lip. Then there were his clothes. He appeared to be wearing a light brown sack. But the man's voice soothed Eddie. He felt safe, somehow. Eddie groaned and lay back down again. He'd just remembered the bright red dragon.

'I must have been seeing things,' he groaned.

The bright red dragon peered over the man's shoulder. 'How is the boyo?' it asked.

Eddie fainted again. It seemed the most logical thing to do.

*

Now, I'm such a quiet narrator that you've probably forgotten all about me, so I hope that it doesn't come as too much of a shock if I stop the action, introduce myself – Hello, reader dearest, I'm the very lovely Philip Ardagh, remember? – and tell you a little bit about where Eddie-who's-forgotten-that-he-*is*-Eddie had ended up. He was in the vast medieval pile of Lamberley Monastery. The monastery was originally built in the year 1074 by Abbot Grynge ('Abbot' being his job title rather than a first name). Of course, he didn't do any of the actual building himself. He was an abbot, not a stonemason or a general dogsbody/gopher/serf/fetcher-and-carrier. He had other people to do all the hard work for him. He was a distant relative of a guy named Bishop Odo who, in turn, was the half-brother of William the Conqueror. And William the Conqueror (once he'd conquered) became King William I of England. This meant that Odo could do pretty much what he wanted to do – until, that is, William threw him in jail in 1082 for plotting against him – and so, as a member of Odo's family, Abbot Grynge would get a lot of favours, too.

People weren't going to argue with Grynge because he could either say: 'I'm going to get my distant cousin's half-brother's army on to you', or 'I'll get the Pope on to you.' Either way, Abbot Grynge was not a man to be messed with.

According to the *Lamberley Chronicles* (written by monks some two hundred years later), 'he was a man of great humbleness and consideration'. According to a piece of graffiti scratched into the monastery stonework in 1089, Grynge was 'a fatty'. What is known for sure, though, is that Abbot Grynge refused to listen to advice not to build his brand-spanking-new monastery where he did. There are a number of bogs, quagmires, marshes and areas of generally 'soft ground' in the vicinity (see *Dreadful Acts*), and Grynge's monastery was built on one of them. Within twenty years or so of the final tile being placed on the roof, the whole thing began to sink. It started at one end, so the whole building had a slight tilt to it, like a ship listing in heavy seas. The result was that if the monks prayed on their knees on the slippery stone floor of the chapel, they found themselves sliding towards the altar like pucks in an ice hockey game. Within a hundred years, the ground floor had become the basement.

By a strange quirk of fate – or, possibly, because God works in mysterious ways – it was the fact that

Lamberley Monastery was built in such a stupid place and suffered the consequences that led to it still standing (even if at a funny angle and partially underground) in Eddie's time. In 1535, another king (Henry VIII) had fallen out with the Pope and decided to get rid of all the monasteries, taking all the land and riches for himself.

According to local tradition, when King Henry's men turned up at Lamberley and saw the funny tilted building in the squishy ground, they assumed that it was already abandoned so didn't bother to destroy it and throw out the monks (who were probably hiding on the floor with all the lights out), and went on their way. The monks just went on living there.

Monks from different orders follow different rules. Two of the most common monastic orders in England – before Henry VIII kicked them out – were the Franciscans and Benedictines. Franciscan monks followed the way of life as laid down by a chap called St Francis of Assisi and Benedictines followed the rules of St Benedict of Nosin. The monks at Lamberley were of the lesser-known Bertian order, founded by Ethelbert the Funny in about 828 AD. Ethelbert the Funny was brother of Ethelbert the Forked-Beard and Ethelbert the Lazy; though why their parents called them *all* Ethelbert escapes me. Perhaps it was a family tradition – there's no record of their father's name – or perhaps the Ethelberts' parents were completely lacking in imagination.

There is a theory that, because in those days the majority of children died before reaching adulthood, their parents expected at least two Ethelberts to die anyway and for them to be left with just the one. *The Lamberley Chronicles* (which I've already mentioned, I'm sure) state that Ethelbert the Lazy died in adulthood, when he couldn't be bothered to get out of the way of a rampaging sheep (which, in turn, dislodged a human-squashingly-large boulder), and that Ethelbert the Forked-Beard later shaved off his beard and became Ethelbert the Clean-Shaven. But, for obvious reasons, it's Ethelbert the Funny with whom the chronicles are most interested.

This particular Ethelbert was given the nickname 'the Funny' on the basis of one joke which, sad to say, isn't even the remotest bit funny by today's standards. Life can be like that. Once Ethelbert was outside his family hovel picking vegetables from a three-foot square strip of soil – remember that: *three-foot* square – which he'd carefully de-stoned, sieved, composted and weeded, when the local baron's henchman appeared in the lane, leading a large horse. The henchman wandered over to Ethelbert. The horse, which must have been bored and had its mind on other things, stepped on Ethelbert's feet with one of its huge iron-shod hooves.

Pulling the horse off, the baron's henchman was most apologetic. 'Are your feet damaged?' he asked.

Ethelbert looked down at his trampled tiny three-foot vegetable patch, and sighed. 'All three feet,' he said, and the legend of Ethelbert the Funny was born.

Geddit? Not that there's much to get. Anyway, that must have been what passed as great humour in the ninth century because, as well as having broken toes, Bert – oh, go on, let's call him Bert now – got his nickname. But how did he get from being one of three Ethelberts living with his mum and dad in a hovel to founding an order of monks? He had a vision, of course. This was a staunchly Christian country and most people who had visions had Christian ones; the Virgin Mary appearing unto them and that kind of thing.

For Bert, it was a little bit different. One day a vegetable spoke to him and tried to lead him into temptation, but Bert guessed that the vegetable was actually the Devil in disguise and rejected his advances. At least, that's how he told it. People were soon flocking from far and wide to come and meet him, and/or to see the vegetable patch. Soon people sought his opinion on everything from the best time to plant runner beans to complicated theological matters.

On his thirty-third birthday he founded his first Bertian monastery, in Yorkshire. The Bertian monks grew the best vegetables of all the local monasteries and told the funniest jokes (which was a bit of a cheat because some monasteries were silent orders where the monks weren't permitted to speak). The years passed, Bert died, but Bertian monasteries sprang up in various parts of the British Isles, but never mainland Europe.

Abbot Grynge chose to follow the Bertian order and built his monastery in Lamberley because he too enjoyed a good vegetable and a good joke and was of the opinion that other orders took life a bit too seriously.

Over the centuries, efforts were made to shore up Lamberley Monastery, and various buildings were added, knocked down or altered but, whatever its shape or size, the monastery continued its slow descent into the boggy ground.

Life in a typical medieval monastery was hard, with long hours and lots of chanting. Monks got to live in fine stone buildings rather than peasants' hovels and the food and drink was usually pretty good, but it was no easy option. Life for monks of the Bertian order was a bit different. Although there were strict rules about wearing scratchy monks' habits of a particular shade of brown, the wearing of humorous undergarments beneath them was actively encouraged.

Who knows what brightly coloured garments the most recent abbot, Abbot Po, had on under his habit as he dabbed Eddie's face with a wet cloth? Whatever they were, I doubt they could have competed with his extraordinary features. I know

I've already told you that his nose was big and warty . . . but 'big' and 'warty' are relative terms. If you're an ant – and if you really *are* an ant, by the way, congratulations on your reading skills (or on your listening skills if you're having this read to you) – then a stag beetle would seem big, but a stag beetle seems tiny if you're an elephant. (And if you're an elephant, please don't sit on me.) By the same token, if you've never had a wart, you may consider someone with one or two warts as being warty . . . but, when all is said and done, Abbot Po's nose was, by human standards, not only GIGANTIC but also warty beyond the normal terms of the definition. Add his protruding upper peg-like teeth and you will, no doubt, agree that he wasn't conventionally handsome. (If you like warty big-nosed folk with peg teeth, however, you'd probably have found him a real treat to the eye.)

What no one who met Abbot Po ever argued about was that he had a beautiful voice. It was soft and gentle and comforting and reassuring and a whole host of other nice and soothing things besides. It sounded like kindness itself.

'What's your name?' he asked Eddie when the boy's eyelids flickered open. 'Can you tell me your name?'

'I'm . . . I – er – don't remember,' Eddie groaned, craning his neck forward as he tried to sit up.

45

'It doesn't matter,' said Abbot Po, still dabbing Eddie's forehead with the cloth. 'It'll come back to you. Now lie still.'

'Where am I?' asked Eddie.

'Somewhere where you'll be well looked after,' the monk assured him.

'The dragon?' asked Eddie. 'There really was a dragon, wasn't there?'

'There was and there wasn't,' said Abbot Po. 'You weren't imagining things, if that's what you were wondering. What you saw was Brother Hyams dressed as a dragon.'

'Why . . . ?'

'Why was he dressed as a dragon? Because he's Welsh, you see,' said Abbot Po, as though it made sense (which, as you'll discover, it did).

'Ned,' said Eddie.

'Ned?' asked the monk.

'Ned,' said Eddie. 'I . . . I – er – think it's my name.'

'Oh, Ned,' nodded Po. 'Good –'

'Or Neddie,' added Eddie, suddenly feeling less sure of himself.

'Or Neddie,' Abbot Po nodded. 'Well, why don't we call you Neddie until you remember whether it is Neddie, or Ned or something completely different altogether?'

Now it doesn't take a great leap in imagination to

46

see how Eddie ended up thinking his name was Neddie, what with being called Eddie and having recently read a book about Ned Kelly after whom he'd named the baby in the bulrushes. It's a small step from Eddie to Neddie. If only he or Abbot Po had realised just *how* close it was to his actual name.

'Well, my name is Po. Abbot Po,' said the monk.

'You're a monk?' asked Eddie.

'A monk,' agreed Abbot Po.

'So Brother Hyams is the only one in fancy dress?'

'In costume,' said the monk. 'We're taking part in the annual Lamberley Pageant. Brother Hyams always dresses as a red dragon, it being the national symbol of Wales. Other brothers will be wearing other costumes on the day. It's one of our rare trips into the local community in such numbers.'

Eddie sat up. 'I must go . . . There's something important I should be doing . . . I'm sure of it . . .'

'Where will you go?' asked Abbot Po. 'Do you know where you live?'

'I . . . er . . . I don't remember anything,' said Eddie, which wasn't strictly true. He's just had a rather confusing image of a giant wooden cow – yes, a giant wooden cow – with a chimney toppling off the top of it. He decided not to mention this to the monk.

'Your trap was damaged beyond repair, I'm afraid to say,' said Abbot Po, 'but, I'm pleased to report that your horse seems fine. He has a nasty cut between his eyes, but no broken bones and Brother Felch will take good care of him. We've stabled him with our horses. We didn't find any belongings in the wreckage of your accident and no clue as to your identity.'

'I wonder if I've travelled far?' said Eddie.

'And whether you were travelling in the direction of your home or away from it,' added Abbot Po. 'From the tracks in the mud where your horse and trap left the road, it's clear that you were coming from the direction of Charlington.

'Charlington?' said Eddie. 'The name doesn't sound familiar.' He'd had another strange fleeting image; this time of a stoat in a stovepipe hat, spitting like a cobra. *That can't be right!* Then he had another thought, and burst out laughing. 'I've just remembered something!' he said.

'What?' asked the monk.

'That 'po' is another name for a chamber pot!' said Eddie. Then he fainted again. This was becoming a habit.

Episode 5

Getting to Know You

In which we recall a couple of Greats, and encounter the author dressed as a chicken

After a remarkably good night's sleep in a guest cell – he wasn't a prisoner, all of the single rooms in the monastery were called cells – Eddie (who thought he was a Neddie, remember) was led to the refectory to meet the other monks.

The refectory was a huge dining hall and, when he and Abbot Po entered, Eddie was faced with one long table running almost the entire length of the room, with a row of monks on benches on either side. They were all dressed almost identically: in light brown habits with slightly pointy-looking hoods.

Eddie was amazed by the noise that greeted him; not the talking – there was none – but the clattering of pewter spoons on pewter plates as hundreds of monks guzzled their breakfast porridge.

'Brothers!' said Abbot Po loudly, attracting their attention. The clattering came to a stop and hundreds of pairs of eyes turned to look at him and the newcomer. 'This is Neddie. He suffered an accident yesterday and is currently in our care.'

'GREETINGS, NEDDIE!' said all the monks as one, their faces breaking into a smile. (Don't forget that the order had been founded by Ethelbert the *Funny*. As monks go, they were an outwardly cheerful lot.)

'G-Greetings,' said Eddie, a little weakly. He was quite a sight to behold. As well as all the little puncture marks all over him, from all those gorse bush prickles (which would have looked very unsightly in the illustrations had Mr Roberts bothered to draw any) he was also walking with the aid of a stick, having hurt the knee and ankle of his left leg. The most noticeable result of his accident, however, was the iodine-soaked bandage wrapped around his head. It looked like a yellowish turban. The overall effect was that Eddie resembled a pantomime street beggar: an exotic but sorry sight.

'Have a seat,' said the nearest monk and all the others on his side of the table shunted down the bench to make room for him. Eddie looked to Po who nodded. The monks on the other side shunted down to make room for him opposite Eddie. They both sat.

Two monks on breakfast duty – Eddie was to discover later that every brother took it in turns to do most tasks in Lamberley Monastery – gave them a plate and a spoon each, then doled out great splodges of porridge with a huge ladle. A large earthenware jar of clear honey and a bowl of rich brown sugar were passed down the table to them.

As Eddie sprinkled his porridge with sugar he frowned.

'What is it?' asked Abbot Po.

'I don't see how I can remember how to walk and talk and eat porridge and things like that, but not remember things about me . . . about my past. I know the days of the week, but I don't know who I am!'

'Don't worry,' said Po. 'It'll all come back to you in time.'

'And there's the noise.'

'The noise?'

'I can distinctly remember the noise of a – er – stuffed stoat hitting the knees of a bearded stranger.'

'A stoat?' said Po.

'A bearded stranger?' asked the monk on Eddie's immediate right.

'Y-Yes.' said Eddie. 'I know it sounds crazy,' (he'd got that right) 'but I'm sure of it . . . No, hang on, I think the stranger turned out to be the Empress of All China.'

A look passed between the monks within earshot: a look which seemed to say *'The poor boy's rambling. The bonk on the head must have been more serious than you thought'*. Those of you familiar with the events outlined in *Awful End*, however, will probably have realised that he was recalling the noise made when Mad Aunt Maud – for this was back in the days before she'd officially become known as Even Madder Aunt Maud – hit the heavily-disguised actor-manager of a group of wandering theatricals named Mr Pumblesnook in the knees with Malcolm (or was it Sally?) her stuffed stoat . . . the self-same actor-manager who later went on to assume the role of a Chinese Empress.

So Eddie wasn't really rambling at all. It was just that he couldn't fill in the blanks to make sense of it. (Not that the events in *Awful End* make a great deal of sense anyway.)

The awful crunching noise of stoat on kneecap was obviously such a remarkable one that it would take more than a serious loss of memory to remove it from young Neddie's – sorry, that should be young *Eddie's* – mind.

I did once mention in passing that this was a noise which Eddie would remember right up until his sixteenth birthday, and that his finally forgetting it had something to do with a hypnotist called the Great Gretcha, not to be confused with an escapologist called the Great Zucchini. (Well, you can see how the confusion might arise; they're both '-ists' by profession and both 'Great' by name.) The Great Gretcha, whom Eddie was to meet a number of years *after* this Further Adventure (having met the Great Zucchini a number of years *prior* to this one), was an American stage hypnotist of German extraction.

Unfortunately, by the time she'd picked out Eddie from a number of arm-waving would-be volunteers in the audience, and had called him up on to the New York stage halfway through her act, she was past her prime. In truth, the night of their meeting was the very last of her professional career.

Poor Gretcha suffered from an illness called narcolepsy which meant that she could suddenly fall asleep without warning – even mid-sentence – which she did with increasing regularity. The show in which Eddie was called up on to the stage, and 'put under' (as hypnotists describe it when a volunteer is put under their hypnotic influence) was her last because, having put him under, she fell asleep . . . leaving him hypnotised.

It was a deep sleep and, once the curtains had been hurriedly lowered and the angry audience promised their money back by the nervous theatre proprietor (a Mr Dundas), they had to awaken the no-longer-so-Great Gretcha in order for *her* to awaken Eddie. By the time she'd snapped him out of his trance, there were one or two gaps in his memory, and the horrible crunch that greeted his ears the day Malcolm and Mr Pumblesnook had made contact was wiped away.

When I told this tale to a well-known stage hypnotist, he insisted that such a thing wasn't possible; that a hypnotist can neither make people do what they don't want to do, nor forget what they don't want to forget. I'm simply stating the facts as they came to me. And, anyway, after my conversation with this chap, I found that I was dressed as a chicken and had no recollection as to how or *why*.

And, now that you've seen what I look like dressed as a chicken (or is it more of a speckledy hen?), my work here is done, so let's return to Lamberley Monastery, to the refectory, to this end of the table and to Eddie with a fine sprinkling of rich brown sugar on his porridge. He was deep in conversation with a plump jolly-looking monk who reminded him of a picture of Friar Tuck he'd once seen in a book about the adventures of Robin Hood and his Merry Men. But *when* had he seen it? Why, where and how? Had the book been his or someone else's? Perhaps it belonged to a brother or sister . . . if he had brothers or sisters. If only he could remember. It was so *frustrating*!

The monk introduced himself as Brother Pugh (like Brother Hyams, a Welshman). 'P-U-G-H, but pronounced *pew*, like the benches,' he said (referring to the name for those wooden seats you find in churches). After breakfast, it was he who took Eddie-he-thought-of-as-Neddie outside to get some fresh air.

They started off by walking around the cloisters. When first constructed, the cloisters had been a covered walkway built around a quadrangle; a large square area of grass. Over the years, though, most of the cloisters had sunk into the ground, so the stone floor had long since disappeared under the earth and the high vaulted ceiling of the cloister now seemed very low indeed. In fact, in some places, Brother Pugh had to duck to avoid hitting his head.

There were various doorways off the cloister leading to the abbey, the Chapter House, a private chapel, and the like, but Pugh led Eddie through an open archway into the herb garden.

A very small elderly monk was making his way along a brick path towards them. He had a large well-worn leather-bound book in his hand which Eddie assumed was either a Bible or a book of herbs. When he got nearer, though, Eddie could read the title in faded embossed gold on the cover: The Bertian Bumper Book Of Funnies. These guys obviously took their jokes very seriously indeed.

Now I'm sure the more caring amongst you are concerned as to the fate that befell Eddie's father, Mr Dickens, when Eddie failed to return with a doctor, so let me put your minds at rest. Or, at the very least, furnish you with the facts (which is a little like furnishing a room but, instead of using tables and chairs, using bits of information. And there's no room involved. Or heavy lifting).

The Dickens household waited and waited and waited and, when neither Eddie nor Dr Humple appeared, and Mr Dickens's groans grew louder and louder and louder, Even Madder Aunt Maud decided to take matters into her own hands.

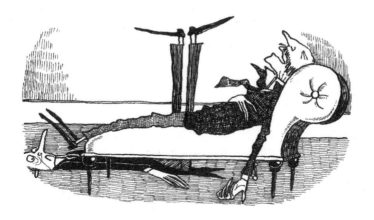

The dear lady knew little about caring for the sick or injured but remembered having heard or read somewhere about a boy called Jack who'd gone up a hill with a girl named Jill in order to fetch a pail of water. As a result, Jack had received a head injury (having then fallen down the hill), and he had been treated with vinegar and brown paper.

Even Madder Aunt Maud instructed Mrs Dickens to go to the kitchen to find vinegar. (They rarely used it on food or in cooking, but Mrs Dickens was a firm believer in using it as a cleaning agent. She insisted that windows, table-tops and even MUJ's ex-soldiers were regularly scrubbed down with the stuff.) Even Madder Aunt Maud, meanwhile, went in search of brown paper.

Brown paper was the kind of paper used to wrap parcels when sending items through the post (usually tied up with hairy string). Mad Uncle Jack was in the habit of paying for items with dried fish, which the local tradespeople then wrapped up in brown paper and sent back to Awful End along with a bill of sale, where Mr Dickens then sent them actual money for their goods and services. He kept the dried fish in a cupboard (for his uncle to re-use) and the brown paper and string in the drawers of the desk in his study.

It was to Mr Dickens's study that Even Madder Aunt Maud now went. She would sometimes spend time annoying her nephew whilst he was trying to sort out the bills, by a variety of different means. Sometimes she would simply hum loudly or shout out random numbers when he was trying to add up a column of figures in his head. Sometimes she would stand behind the curtains and stick Malcolm's head out with a cheery, 'Peekaboo!'. Occasionally, she'd drink the water from the vases, gargling loudly before each swallow. If this failed to gain Mr Dickens's attention, she'd sometimes end up eating the flowers in the vase, too. (They'd die soon anyway, once she'd drunk the water.)

It was whilst she'd been involved in such activities that she'd spotted where he kept the brown paper, so now she was able to go straight to the relevant desk drawers and to gather it by the armful.

Hurrying back to the *chaise longue* where Mr Dickens lay, she almost collided with Mrs Dickens who was carrying an enormous earthenware jar of home-made chutney.

'I couldn't find the vinegar,' Mrs Dickens explained.

'I'm sure that'll do nicely,' said EMAM.

They proceeded to cover Mr Dickens with the apple-based chutney and then applied the brown paper (the chutney acting as a remarkably effective glue, in much the same way that the marmalade had on the breakfast plate).

Somewhat surprisingly, Mr Dickens found the treatment quite soothing. So much so, that his wife and aunt decided to try the same healing approach on Dawkins, still bent double from his 'locked' back. Unfortunately for the gentleman's gentleman, they only succeeded in attracting a swarm of bees that stung him repeatedly, whilst he was in no fit state to run away.

In all this excitement, Eddie's absence was put to the back of everyone's mind.

The Game's Afoot

*In which Fandango Jones plays detective and
Even Madder Aunt Maud plays the bagpipes*

Whilst the others were concerned with Mr Dickens's injuries, Fandango Jones had been investigating the scene of the crime, for that's what he was sure that it was: a *crime*. He was convinced that the chimney falling on Mr Dickens had been no accident. Perhaps Mr Dickens hadn't been the intended target, but the engineer was sure that the chimney had been deliberately dropped from the roof of Awful End on to the cluster of people below, which was why it was on the roof that Fandango was now standing.

The little man was re-checking the calculations he'd made from the ground and had reached the same conclusion. There was no way that the chimney could have landed, or even been pushed, from its original position and fallen where it had. Someone must have lifted the chimney on to or over the parapet and pushed, dropped or thrown it over the edge! And whoever had done that must have seen the members of the household below, so *must* have intended them harm.

'Most interesting,' said the engineer, for he was one of the very few people in the world who really did speak to himself out loud (unlike characters in books, who seem to do it all the time).

Fandango Jones was used to standing on tall things because he'd built so many of them. He built the Tottering Tower at Totteridge, for example, and the Scarbourne Lighthouse. I wouldn't be surprised if you haven't heard of either of them – unless you live in Totteridge or Scarbourne, and are interested in local history – because neither is still standing. They both fell down a long time ago. Quite a few of Fandango Jones's taller structures did, many in his lifetime; a fact not mentioned in his pamphlet *Bridging the Gap*.

Jones was about to go back through the tiny doorway which led to and from this section of roof – Awful End was a very higgledy-piggledy building with roofs of different heights and designs – when something caught his eye: a flash of colour against the grey of the stone edging. He went to investigate and picked up a piece of faded gold brocade (a rich fabric woven with a raised pattern, like you used to get on military uniforms). It was caught on a peg holding a damaged roof tile in place.

Perhaps the person who'd dropped the chimney over the edge had snagged his clothing on the peg when walking past.

Fandango Jones slipped the brocade into the back of his notebook for safekeeping. This looked very much like a clue to him.

As he walked back down the winding staircase to the top landing, he wondered about the chimney itself. If it had been a statue or a stone urn that had been pushed over, that could have been a spur of the moment thing. It needn't have been planned. Whoever it was could have been looking over the edge and thought, 'I know, I'll flatten one of those Dickenses today,' and then pushed the object over. But not with the chimney. The chimney would have to have been dislodged from its original position on top of the stack – it was one of a cluster of four barley-sugar chimneys sharing a base – and then carried to the edge and over the parapet. Premeditated. That was what they called it in those detective magazines Jones liked to read: 'a premeditated act'. The dropping of the chimney had been pre-planned. Fandango Jones hadn't been this excited since . . . since he'd got all enthusiastic about the suggestion of a bridge made of soup (until he'd come to his senses).

Jones hurried into the nearest room – about two-thirds of the rooms in Awful End were unused, and most without furniture, remember – sat himself on an old hatbox, and immediately started drawing a diagram. Sadly, this no longer exists but, based on a description from the son of someone who actually saw the original, here's David Roberts's reconstruction of what it looked like:

Thanks, David. Not bad.

By the time Jones had finished his diagram and made his way back downstairs to the others, a few of them were beginning to wonder, if not worry exactly, about the whereabouts of Eddie and the doctor.

Unaware of the calamitous events resulting in both Mr Dickens and Dawkins lying flat on their backs in the withdrawing room, Gibbering Jane had emerged from below stairs with a happy baby Ned gurgling in her arms, to ask the whereabouts of Master Edmund. At the mention of his name, it was the general consensus that he should, indeed, have returned by now.

'Perhaps he's been kidnapped by escaped convicts up on the misty moors,' suggested Mad Uncle Jack.

'Unlikely,' snapped Even Madder Aunt Maud.

'Or been mistaken for an escaped orphan and locked in a police cell,' MUJ added.

Even Madder Aunt Maud poo-pooed that suggestion too.

'Or stuck himself to the underside of a circus elephant,' said Mad Uncle Jack, going all misty-eyed at the memory of when his own dear wife had done that very thing many years previously.

Even Madder Aunt Maud threw her arms around him, showering him with slobbery kisses from her prune-like lips. 'You remember, my love pumpkin!' she cried.

Mrs Dickens turned away. Not only was this not a pretty sight, but she'd also been side-swiped, in the face, by Malcolm – or was it Sally? – whom Maud was clutching when she threw her arms around her Jack. She decided to go and find something to lessen the bruising.

Gibbering Jane was now in the withdrawing room, gibbering at the sight of poor Dawkins, covered in bee stings, doing a very good impersonation of a right angle. Baby Ned seemed to find the gibbering amusing, and his face broke into a gummy smile. He dribbled with pleasure.

The not-so-famous engineer, meanwhile, went in search of Mad Uncle Jack and Even Madder Aunt Maud. He found them emerging from a broom cupboard.

'The family chapel is much smaller than I recall,' Eddie's great-aunt was saying.

Mad Uncle Jack grunted in agreement. 'Perhaps the whole house is shrinking.'

Even Madder Aunt Maud nodded. 'It did rain a great deal in the winter,' she said, 'and water does shrink things. Remember your brother George. He shrank in that fish tank, didn't he?'

Even Madder Aunt Maud was referring to George Dickens who took to living in a fish tank in a rented space near what is now the Victoria & Albert Museum in London.

'He didn't shrink, my sweet,' said Mad Uncle Jack. 'He drowned.' Which was also true. Refusing to come up for air one day – a Thursday – he did, indeed, drown. This was the same George Dickens who accidentally burnt down the Houses of Parliament in 1834. (You can read all about it in my book *Terrible Times* . . . if you haven't already done so, that is.)

'But he could have shrunk a bit before he drowned,' EMAM pointed out.

At this stage, Fandango Jones cleared his throat to let the couple know that he was there.

When Even Madder Aunt Maud spotted him, she let out a yelp. 'It's the spitting man!' she cried, leaping behind her husband to use him as a human shield.

'I thought you were the engineer,' said a puzzled Mad Uncle Jack.

'Indeed I am, sir,' said Fandango, 'but it's in the capacity of amateur detective that I must speak with you now.'

'Then spit it out, man!' said Mad Uncle Jack. 'What's troubling you?'

'Be quick about it, mind,' said EMAM. 'This house is shrinking and something must be done!'

'You were in the broom cupboard, madam,' he said.

'I beg your pardon?'

'You weren't in the chapel. That is through the door over there.' He pointed. (Mrs Dickens had given him a tour of Awful End when he'd undertaken to build the bridge in its grounds.) 'You and your husband entered the broom cupboard in error.'

'Are you trying to tell me that I don't know the Dickens family chapel when I see it?' demanded Even Madder Aunt Maud.

'Are you suggesting that we don't know a place for storing brooms from a house of God?' Mad Uncle Jack bellowed, his beakiest of beaky noses quivering with rage.

Fandango Jones squirmed. He'd never seen his employer so angry, and this had been of *his* making. 'I – er –'

'This is outrageous,' Mad Uncle Jack shouted, turning to the broom cupboard and yanking open the door. 'Are you telling me that this doesn't contain some of the finest examples of wood carving since Grinning Gibbons?' (None of them, including Mad Uncle Jack, had any idea who Grinning Gibbons was.)

Fandango Jones didn't know what to say. Certainly the family chapel at Awful End – which was just behind that wall, there – had some very fine wooden carvings . . . but the only wood he could see in this dingy cupboard were the handles of the mops and brooms, and (rather oddly) a small log next to a large piece of rock.

'Er, very nice,' he said lamely.

Mad Uncle Jack looked in the cupboard. 'Great heavens!' he said. 'It's nothing but a broom cupboard.'

'What did you think it was?' Even Madder Aunt Maud snorted. 'A slice of cheese?'

'It's your nephew –' said the engineer, in a desperate bid to steer the conversation back to the fallen chimney.

'My nephew is a broom cupboard?'

'A slice of cheese?'

'Preposterous!'

'Ridiculous!'

'No . . .' protested Fandango Jones. 'It's your

nephew, Mr Dickens, about whom I must speak!'

'Spit, more like,' said Even Madder Aunt Maud.

Jones felt happier to be back on more familiar ground. 'I believe that the accident with the chimney was no accident at all.'

'Then why refer to it as an accident?' asked EMAM.

'Exactly!' said MUJ. 'Are you some kind of an idiot? A buffoon?'

Jones tried again. 'I meant, of course, that which we *took* to be an accident was no accident at all. I believe that the chimney was deliberately dropped upon our party below.'

'Party? I don't recall a party,' protested Even Madder Aunt Maud. 'Where were the jellies? The ices? The most-amusing of party games?'

'Party as in assembled group, madam,' spat Jones. 'I believe that the chimney was deliberately dropped upon us and is, therefore, a case of attempted murder . . . and a matter for the police!'

There always seems to be police involvement in an Eddie Dickens adventure, doesn't there?

Caped Capers

*In which the author makes an apology
and Brother Gault makes a potion*

et me start by way of an apology. It's not the first one I've had to make and I doubt it'll be the last. So here goes: Some of you will have spotted that the previous chapter begins with the lead-in: '*In which Fandango Jones plays detective and Even Madder Aunt Maud plays the bagpipes.*' Well, we certainly had the Fandango-Jones-playing-detective part (what with his diagrams and clue-collecting, and clambering about the roof), but what about Even Madder Aunt Maud and the bagpipes? Now if it had said, '*In which Fandango Jones plays detective and Even Madder Aunt Maud plays the fool*' or even, '*plays about in a broom cupboard*' that would have been fine. But '*plays the bagpipes?*' I think not!

You see, the thing is, I was going to get to the part where Maud plays the bagpipes and then I thought, NO! HANG ON! THAT'LL HAVE TO WAIT! This book is the second of the Further Adventures of *Eddie Dickens*, so I think we should get back to Eddie – even though he doesn't know that he's Eddie, of course – and we can come back to Even Madder Aunt Maud and her bagpipe-playing later on. OK? OK. Good. Thank you for being so understanding.

So back to Eddie we go. A good few days had passed and the pock marks where the gorse bush prickles had been pulled out were a lot less painful, and the yellowing iodine-soaked bandages had been unwound from his head. He did, however, still have to walk with a stick, and his memory hadn't come back.

That's not to say that certain memories hadn't returned in fleeting flashes, including riding on the back of a turtle . . . removing a large sparkling bauble from a chandelier . . . leading a gang of scruffily-dressed, cucumber-wielding children out of a grim building . . . digging up a coffin with his bare hands . . . but none of them seemed to make any sense or give him a clue as to who he was.

Abbot Po had deduced from Eddie's clothing,

accent and horse that 'Neddie' was from the well-to-do classes but, beyond that, nothing.

One of the problems was that, except for rare occurrences, such as taking part in the up-coming Lamberley Pageant (which would require Brother Hyams to dress as a Welsh dragon), the Bertians had little to do with the world around them. They were what's known as a 'slightly ajar order'.

A closed order (of monks or nuns) is one that has no dealings with the outside world. Then there are the open orders that go out in the community (to do good deeds, I suppose). A slightly ajar order is one that is more closed than open, but not completely closed. In other words, Bertian monks in general, including the monks at Lamberley Monastery, usually kept people out and out of people's way, except when it suited them.

This appears to have meant that, in the case of Eddie's accident, it was only right and Christian to rescue the injured boy and his injured horse, when he was spotted by the side of the road, but not necessarily to involve the authorities. So they didn't.

Eddie had quickly adapted to life in the monastery. He didn't go to all the prayers the monks attended throughout the day but sometimes he sat at the back of the chapel and listened to the brothers chant and sink. Sorry, that should be *sing*. Of course, the building was sinking, but not right before their very eyes. Not then, at least. Everyone was terribly nice to Eddie/Neddie and he was eager to help out around the place as much as possible: in the kitchens, on the land, or wherever he could lend a hand.

Brother Gault, the herbalist, concocted a potion designed to speed Eddie's recovery and he took a spoonful each morning and a spoonful each night. This may not sound a very high dosage until you see the size of the spoon (which you probably have done if you looked at the picture first). It was the biggest wooden spoon Eddie had ever seen in his life, not that he could remember any of the other wooden spoons he'd seen. Fortunately, the medicine tasted rather nice, as medicines go, and this one went in his mouth and down his front.

Another thing you might have noticed from the picture is that Eddie was now wearing a habit. It's not that they were insisting Eddie become a Bertian novice or anything like that. (A novice is a monk in training.) It was just that Eddie had only one set of clothes and they weren't in the best of condition since his accident anyway.

Eddie's habit had been made-to-measure from an old (much larger) garment by Brother Henry, who was very good at sewing. Because Eddie wasn't really a monk it didn't have a proper hood but, apart from that, it was just like the clothes everyone else wore at Lamberley Monastery (except that, unlike the others, Eddie wasn't wearing humorous undergarments). It felt very rough and itchy.

'Do you think I'll ever find out who I am?' he asked Abbot Po in the monastery library, after breakfast one morning.

'I'm sure you'll be home again in no time,' replied Po in his kindly voice. 'When we attend the pageant, I've no doubt someone will come forward and claim you.'

'I do hope so,' said Eddie. 'Please don't misunderstand me, Abbot Po. No one could be kinder to me than you and the other monks, and there's no place I'd rather be with a loss of memory than here, except for home . . .'

'But home is where the heart is,' Abbot Po nodded in understanding. 'Even if you don't know where home is.'

'Or who's in it,' Eddie added.

'Which is why I've given instructions that should any of the brothers have reason to be out in the community, they should make enquires about you.'

'How do you mean?' asked Eddie.

'I mean,' Po explained, 'that it is against the orders of our order to walk into a police station and to report you missing, but if one of my brothers should be out selling our vegetables and happens to ask if anyone had heard reports of a missing boy –'

'Then that is all right.'

'Then that is, indeed, perfectly acceptable,' said Abbot Po.

'You monks have funny rules, don't you?' said Eddie, hurriedly adding: 'No disrespect, abbot.'

'None taken,' said Po. 'You're forgetting that our order was founded by Ethelbert the Funny.'

A few moments later, Brother Hyams entered the monastery library. 'It's the sheep, Abbot Po!' he said. 'I'm afraid they've got out again.'

★

Just a few miles away, as the crow flies (if the crow is concentrating and hasn't been sidetracked by a juicy worm he's spotted far below, or been blown off course on to the misty moors) a Bertian monk by the name of Brother Guck was trudging his way up the ever-so-long driveway of a very impressive house indeed. He knocked on the door.

No sooner had his knuckles left the wood than the door was flung wide open and the startled Bertian was confronted by an elderly woman playing the bagpipes. (Yup: b-a-g-p-i-p-e-s.)

'What is it?' she demanded, letting the bag deflate with a painful whine.

'Sheep, madam,' said Guck. 'I am here about our sheep.'

'Why would I wish to buy sheep?' demanded Even Madder Aunt Maud – for, as you guessed, it was she – peering around the tall thin monk to see whether he had brought any samples of his wares with him.

'I'm not selling them, madam,' the young monk explained.

'Good!' said EMAM, 'because I found two perfectly good sheep grazing outside my cow this morning, so I now have more than enough.'

'But those are the very sheep I'm referring to, madam,' said Brother Guck, wondering what she'd meant by *outside her cow*. 'They strayed from monastery land. They belong to the monastery. I am here to –'

76

'Finders keepers!' Eddie's great-aunt stated with a haughty chuckle.

'Whilst I'm here,' the monk added hurriedly, 'I should also mention a lost boy whom, we believe, is named Ned –'

'Why didn't you say so in the first place?' said the elderly woman, throwing the bagpipes with great force into the fireplace. 'You're here about Ned?'

'You know him?' asked Guck. He and his fellow monks had been visiting various neighbouring properties to round up the sheep, but none of the others knew anything about a missing boy.

'I certainly do! You've come to the right place,' said Even Madder Aunt Maud. 'He was like Moses in the bulrushes. Have you heard of him?'

'I most certainly have, madam,' said the monk.

'He's in the Bible, you know.'

'I know,' nodded the brother.

'Then follow me!' said the strange old lady, picking up what appeared to be a stuffed ferret or weasel or stoat off an occasional table.

Slightly bemused – which is like puzzled but with less 'z's in it – Brother Guck followed the old lady through a large hall where he couldn't fail to notice possibly one of the most hideous painted ceilings that he'd ever had the misfortune to clap eyes on: there was something frighteningly *liver-sausagy* about it all.

They finally entered the kitchen where an ex-soldier was standing in a tin bath filled with vinegar, being scrubbed down by Mrs Dickens.

'He's here about young Ned,' said Even Madder Aunt Maud.

'Good morning, madam,' Brother Guck said to Mrs Dickens.

'Good morning,' she replied, dipping a large brush into the iron tub and giving Ex-Private Drabb's back another scrub.

Even Madder Aunt Maud marched over to the drawer in which Baby Ned was peacefully sleeping.

She picked him up and plonked him down in the arms of the startled monk.

'There you go!' she said. 'One missing Ned safely returned to his rightful owner.'

'There must be some mistake –' Guck began.

'You come to my door. You ask about a lost boy named Ned. I give you a found boy named Ned and you say there's some mistake, is that it?' she demanded, her voice rising to a grating pitch.

'I . . . er –'

'You lost a Ned. We found a Ned and you're saying that they're not one and the same? Hmmm? Is that it!?'

At that moment, Mad Uncle Jack ambled in through the back door (having slept and abluted in and around his dried-fish tree house). 'Who the devil are you, sir?' he demanded. 'And what are you doing with that bawling babe?'

'He's come to claim Ned,' said Mrs Dickens above the howls.

'Ned?' asked MUJ.

'That baby we found.'

'Oh, him,' said Mad Uncle Jack. 'Good. Good. Now get off my land before I have you shot.'

It was then that Brother Guck made a decision. He would forget about the two stray sheep that the bagpipe-playing woman had mentioned. He would forget about the other missing boy called Neddie, back at the monastery. He would try not to think about the poor man being given a vinegar bath and about the horrendous ceiling in the hallway. His number one priority in the whole wide world at that precise moment was to get this poor baby out of the madhouse.

'Th-Thank you and good day,' he said, then, cradling the crying child in his arms, made for the nearest exit . . . and found himself in a broom cupboard.

'I suppose you think that's funny?' snapped Even Madder Aunt Maud.

*

Whilst Guck and a group of fellow monks were off scouring the surrounding countryside for the missing sheep, a visitor came to Lamberley Monastery.

He was a stocky, swarthy man with eyes of such a dark brown that they were almost black. He had a large gold tooth at the front of his mouth and a large gold hooped ear-ring in his right ear. He wore a red neckerchief with white spots around – you guessed it – his neck. If it wasn't for the fact that he smelled strongly of horses, one might have supposed that he was a pirate. In truth, he was a gypsy.

Gypsies used to be called *gipcyans* or *gyptians* because people thought that these travelling folk had originally come from Egypt. Many gypsies speak Romany, their own special language which is Indo-European (which means that it's spoken across Europe and Asia as far as northern India), which makes things all the more confusing. This gypsy, however, was called Fudd, and had spent his entire life, man and boy, travelling around the British Isles.

'I'm here about the boy who's lost his memory,' he told the monk who finally opened the door to the monastery gatehouse after it became clear that the gypsy wasn't going to stop banging on it with his knobbly walking stick until somebody did something.

The mention of 'the boy' got a speedy reaction, and it wasn't long before Fudd was taken to see Abbot Po in his office.

'By the Lord, you're ugly!' gasped Fudd when he laid eyes on the warty-nosed peg-toothed monk.

'That's no word of a lie,' agreed Po from behind his desk, 'which is fortunate for you, sir, because it means that I don't judge you by appearances alone.'

'Meaning?' demanded Fudd, his eyes narrowing.

'Meaning that there are those who won't give a gypsy so much as the time of day,' said Po.

'But you're a man of God!' said Fudd. 'It is your duty to like all men.'

'And it's because you're in God's house that I ask you to remove your cap, sir,' said Po, quietly.

The gypsy snatched his hat off the top of his head, mumbling an apology. He and the abbot had got off on the wrong foot.

'Do, please, sit down,' said Abbot Po, indicating towards one of the few comfortable chairs in the whole building.

'Thank you,' said the gypsy. 'And I means no harm by my comments. I speaks my mind, that's all.'

'Admirable if you find someone beautiful, Mr –?'

'Fudd,' said Fudd.

'Mr Fudd, but it's probably best to bite your tongue if you meet someone as hideous as me. Not everyone would be so understanding.'

Fudd grinned. 'Speakin' me mind has lost me a few teeth over the years, but I gives as good as I get.'

'I'm told you're here about a boy?'

'Yes. He went missing from our camp last week sometime.'

Abbot Po leaned forward in his chair. 'And what is the boy's name?' he asked.

''Tis Fabian, sir,' said Fudd. 'His mother's choice.'

'And you are the father?'

'Lord, no,' laughed Fudd. 'I am their chief. Father to 'em all in a way though, I suppose. I also deals with all important business.'

'And what could be more important than a missing child?'

''xactly!' said Fudd. 'When I heard your monks asking around about a child who'd lost his memory, I came straight here.'

'Would you describe Fabian to me, please?' he asked.

Fudd was happy to. He described a boy of Eddie's age, height and appearance. 'He has eyes like saucers,' he finished.

This description of Fabian certainly sounded like the boy he knew as Neddie, but how could he be sure? And then there was the fact that the horse Neddie had been found with appeared to be a *gentleman's* horse, and Eddie spoke like a little gentleman, not at all like Fudd.

'Could you describe his horse?' asked Po.

The gypsy looked down at his lap and wrung his cap in his hands somewhat awkwardly. 'You see, the thing is, sir, that he shouldn't have had no horse with him . . .' he said. 'If you found Fabian with a horse, it weren't his by rights.'

'You're suggesting that he'd stolen it?'

'Now don't get me wrong,' said Fudd. 'We gypsies have a bad reputation as horse thieves and it's mostly unfounded . . . but, if Fabian takes a fancy to a steed, he sometimes feels the need to take it for himself, see?'

'I see,' said Po. He was about to have Neddie brought to his office when something else occurred to him. 'His speech,' he said. 'How does Fabian speak?'

'I'm not sure I follows you,' said Fudd.

'How does he sound? What kind of accent?'

'Aha! I sees where you're heading!' said Fudd. 'I should have said from the outset that the lad speaks real beautifully. He sounds as if he comes from the very best of society.'

'But how did Fabian come to speak this way?' the abbot asked with interest.

'His mother, Hester, weren't born a Romany,' Fudd explained. 'She's an outsider who married into our family. A very well-to-do lady.'

'Unusual,' said Po, but he had no reason to doubt the man. He was now convinced that 'Neddie' was none other than Fabian. 'We must reunite you with Fabian this instant.'

And this is how Eddie, who still thought of himself as Neddie, now came to believe himself to be Fabian. Of course, he didn't recognise Fudd when he was ushered into the office by Brother Pugh but, then again, he wouldn't have recognised Florinda Dickens as his mother nor Laudanum Dickens as his father if they'd been standing there in the gypsy's place.

When Fudd looked up as Eddie entered the room, a flicker of surprise crossed his face, but Abbot Po was too busy looking at Eddie to notice.

'Fabian!' said the gypsy, giving Eddie a hug. 'It's good to see you. Remember me?' he asked.

'I'm afraid not, sir,' said Eddie. 'Are you my father?'

'I'm not, but I'll be taking you back to him,' said Fudd, grinning his golden grin.

On the Case

*In which Fandango Jones
helps the police with their enquiries*

Fandango Jones had been the one who'd volunteered to bicycle to the police station to report his suspicions about the chimney hitting Eddie's father being a case of attempted murder. He also agreed to report Eddie's own disappearance whilst he was at it. But what everyone had forgotten about in the excitement – what with Gibbering Jane being so good at looking after him – was Baby Ned (or whatever his real name was). Had Fandango mentioned his being found in the bulrushes, the baby would probably have been looked after by some local orphanage and not ended up being taken by Brother Guck. So, as things turned out, it's lucky that what Jones was *really* interested in was playing detective with a real live one.

Those of you familiar with the Eddie Dickens Trilogy will also be familiar with the figure of the detective inspector. In the three previous books in which he's appeared, he's only ever been described as being 'the inspector' or 'the detective inspector'. This was for legal reasons which have been dragging on and on and on and on down the years. Now that these have been resolved, I'm happy to give you his full name: Detective Inspector Humphrey Bunyon.

Now there were two very distinct things about the detective inspector. No, come to think of it, there were *three*: one – in no particular order – was that he was prone to repeat what the previous person had just said but, often in such a way that it made a strange kind of sense; two, he couldn't read (which wasn't uncommon at the time, but was more uncommon amongst detective inspectors); and, three, he had a very large tummy indeed. It was gigantic, and looked even more so because of the loud checked suits he always wore.

Well, amazingly, although one (his repetition) and two (his illiteracy) still applied when Fandango Jones went to spit at him that day, number three was no longer true. Detective

Inspector Humphrey Bunyon had been on the ultimate diet – locked in a trunk by a gang of purse snatchers and cut-throats for nearly a month – so was now remarkably slim. This wouldn't have been a problem if the policeman hadn't intended to put the weight back on – he loved his food – so hadn't bothered to buy himself any new clothes. His old ones hung off him like . . . like . . . Well, he looked like a thin man in fat man's clothing.

When the engineer managed to get past the desk sergeant (who was proudly trying out a set of new-fangled handcuffs on himself) he was shocked by the sight of the detective in his extraordinarily baggy clothing.

'Good morning,' said Jones.

'Good morning.'

'Are you the detective inspector?' asked Jones.

'The detective inspector,' nodded Humphrey Bunyon.

'My name is Fandango Jones, the fairly well-known engineer –'

'Fandango Jones, the fairly well-known engineer,' the policeman nodded.

'Perhaps you've heard of me?' said Jones.

'Heard of you,' nodded the detective inspector.

'Excellent!' said Jones, trying not to be distracted by just how strange Bunyon looked with the folds of clothes hanging off him, like the loose skin of a rhinoceros.

'Excellent,' agreed the inspector. 'Why are you here, Mr Jones?' The policeman was seated behind a large desk. In the past, he'd found it difficult to reach for items on his desk because his stomach had kept him more than arm's length away from it. Since he'd escaped from the evil clutches of the Smiley Gang, though, he now found life behind his desk much easier. He picked up a buff-coloured folder, not to read (he didn't know how to, remember) but to use as some form of protection against this *spitting* man.

'I believe that my current employer's nephew has been the victim of an attempted murder!'

'Attempted murder?'

'Attempted murder!' Jones spat.

'Attempted murder? Hmmmm,' said the inspector. 'Please go on.'

Fandango Jones sat on the only chair in the

room (Inspector Bunyon was using a pile of books). 'I am currently constructing a bridge at Awful End,' he said. The policeman said nothing. His face dropped at the very mention of the place. 'My employer's name is Mad Mr Jack Dickens and –'

The detective inspector put up his hand for silence. 'Unfortunately,' he sighed, 'I am familiar with the Dickens household. Do go on.'

So Fandango Jones told him his sorry tale.

Detective Inspector Humphrey Bunyon listened in silence. He was a very good detective inspector and would occasionally interrupt with a question.

When Fandango Jones had finished, the policeman got to his feet, his laughably large clothes making him look like a half-deflated hot-air balloon. 'I do believe you're right,' he said.

'Right?' spat the engineer.

'Right that a person or persons deliberately dropped the chimney on to the gathering below and that Mr Dickens may or may not have been the intended target. And right that Master Edmund Dickens's disappearance may somehow be connected to the affair.'

Fandango Jones glowed with such pride that a piece of his spit which had settled on his chin sizzled in the heat that such a glow can generate.

'So what do you intend to do about it?' he asked.

'Do about it?'

'Do about it,' Jones nodded, his two-tier stovepipe hat wobbling under the strain. Fandango Jones was not a man to take his hat off indoors; especially not one as heavy as this.

'I intend to make immediate enquiries!' said the inspector. He crossed the floor, opened the door to his office and called for his desk sergeant.

'Yes sir?' said the sergeant, entering the room with a somewhat sheepish expression on his face.

'Round up a few constables! I'm going to Awful End.'

'Yes, sir!' said the sergeant but, rather than turning and leaving the room sharpish, he stood with his back to Jones and spoke to the inspector in almost a whisper. 'Only there's something I need to ask you first, sir.'

'What is it?' asked the inspector.

'Keys, sir.'

'Keys?'

'Keys . . . to these handcuffs. You wouldn't happen to have them, would you?'

It was only then, using his police-enhanced powers of observation, that the detective inspector noticed his desk sergeant had managed to lock his wrists together with his own handcuffs.

★

With Fabian . . . I mean Neddie . . . I mean *Eddie* now convinced that he was part of Fudd's band of gypsies, he asked if he could say goodbye to Horsey (whose name he didn't know either), because it was agreed that the animal should stay at the monastery whilst the monks tried to find his 'rightful owner'. Eddie felt strange leaving behind the one link he had with his arrival at the monastery. He went with Abbot Po and the gypsy chief, Fudd, to the stables.

Brother Felch led the horse out into the yard. The nasty cut between Horsey's eyes was healing nicely. 'He'll soon be as fit as a fiddle,' he announced, slipping him a carrot from a bag slung on the rope belt tied around his waist.

Eddie patted him on the muzzle. 'Goodbye, boy,' he said.

It was just as Fudd reached the gatehouse, Eddie hobbling beside him on his stick, that Abbot Po called out after them.

'Just a moment, Mr Fudd!' he said.

Fudd stopped and turned. 'Yes, abbot?'

'I haven't heard you ask young Fabian about his injuries.'

'Beg pardon?' said the gypsy, an uneasy feeling creeping over him.

'You haven't once asked the boy how he is.'

'S'not true,' said Fudd defensively. 'I asked the lad if he remembered me.'

'You enquired about his memory, yes,' said Po, 'but, despite the puncture holes all over him and his walking with a stick, you've never once asked how he's feeling. You, the chief and father to them all.'

'We're manly men, us gypsies,' said Fudd.

'And if this boy really is Fabian and one of your own, I'm sure you'd have asked him about his wellbeing by now.'

'Are you calling me a liar?' asked Fudd, raising his knobbly stick above Po's head.

'I'm simply saying that, before you leave with the boy, I feel that we need more proof that he is who you say he is.'

Now, before we go any further, I think I'd better do a little explaining here. Ready? When Fudd arrived at Lamberley Monastery, he really *was* hoping to find Fabian. It's not that he'd made Fabian up with a view to kidnapping Eddie for some nefarious purposes (and if you're not altogether sure what nefarious actually means, you could always look it up). Fabian existed and he was exactly whom Fudd had said he was: one of the gypsy children whose mother hadn't been born a gypsy but had fallen in love with one and married him. It was just that when Eddie was led into Abbot Po's office and turned out *not* to be the boy, Fudd saw an interesting opportunity. And Fudd was not one to turn down an opportunity in a hurry.

A plan formed very quickly in his mind. He would claim this Neddie as being Fabian, take him away with him and then track down his real parents. There was bound to be a reward, and Fudd would be far better at tracking them down than a bunch of monks who didn't get out much. And he'd still be on the lookout for the *real* Fabian in the meantime.

Clever, huh?

And if you're sitting there/standing there/ squatting there/kneeling there/lying there thinking, 'Poor old gypsies! Here's yet *another* book giving them and travelling people a bad name,' let me say this:

1. Fudd was just Fudd, and was not representative of all gypsies.
2. There are good gypsies and bad gypsies in just the same way that there are good dentists and bad dentists. They're only human. (Bad example. I'm not sure my dentist is.)

3. Eddie came across a wide variety of unsavoury characters over the years, and Fudd the gypsy was just one of them. So, as a percentage of the not-so-marvellous people Eddie encountered, gypsies probably made up less than one per cent.

4. Fudd wasn't that bad anyway!

Enough said.

Fudd lowered his stick. 'I'm sorry, abbot,' he said. 'I had no real intention of hitting you.'

'I'm glad to hear it,' said Po.

'Not just because you're a man of God, but because I don't hit no defenceless man with nothing but me fists.'

'Even one as ugly as me?' asked Po.

''specially one as ugly as you,' grinned the gypsy.

'Is this boy really Fabian?' Po asked, staring straight into the man's eyes.

Fudd blinked and looked away. 'How come God made one so kind and clever as you so ugly?'

'Perhaps to remind us that we shouldn't always judge a book by its cover,' said Po, putting his arm around Eddie's shoulders. 'Come on, Neddie,' he said. 'It looks as though you won't be leaving our company just yet after all.'

'You mean, I'm not this Fabian fellow?' asked Eddie. He turned to Fudd, who shook his head.

'I'm sorry, son. No,' he said. 'Though you are like two peas in a pod. Uncanny it is. Unnatural.'

'Then why –?'

'I'd have found your real folks for you, and no mistake,' he said.

'At a price, I suppose?' said Po.

The gypsy nodded again.

'Good day to you, Mr Fudd,' said Abbot Po briskly.

'You'll be reporting this to the authorities?' asked Fudd, who wasn't on the best of terms with police throughout the country.

It was Po's turn to shake his head. 'I report to the highest authority,' he said, looking skywards. 'If you never return to Lamberley, I have no reason to tell anyone of what happened here.'

'Right . . . Well – er – Good luck with your memory and the like,' said Fudd, then he marched through the gatehouse out into the world.

One of his men was waiting by his horse. 'Was it Fabian, chief?' he asked.

'No,' said Fudd, jumping up on to his animal. 'There's nothing for us here.'

★

By the time Fandango Jones returned to Awful End in the horse-drawn police van (his bicycle slung up on to its roof), Dr Humple had arrived to tend to the wounded.

For someone who'd had a chimney dropped on him from a great height, Mr Dickens was, the doctor declared, in remarkably good condition. Humple had ordered all the chutney and brown paper removed before he could make his initial examination of the patient. Mrs Dickens had managed to get much of the chutney back into the earthenware jar, declaring that it would be 'a shame for it to go to waste', whilst Even Madder Aunt Maud was busy licking what remained stuck to the brown paper.

According to Dr Humple, it was Dawkins who was in need of more immediate attention. 'Time will heal your husband's broken bones, Mrs Dickens,' he said, 'but Dawkins needs those bee stings extracted this instant.'

Feeling a little guilty that it was her applying of the chutney to the gentleman's gentleman that had attracted the swarm of bees in the first place, Mrs Dickens insisted on helping the doctor pull out the stings. Even Madder Aunt Maud, who'd been watching from the sidelines, decided that she wanted a go, too, which is why, on entering the house, Detective Inspector Bunyon found three people attacking Dawkins with tweezers.

Fandango Jones had then taken the policeman and his constables up on to the roof, shown him where the chimney had originally stood, shown him where it must have been dropped over the edge and, leaning over the parapet, pointed out where they'd all been standing below. He then produced the piece of brocade from the back of his notebook and handed it to the inspector, pointing out the exact spot where he'd found it.

'Remarkable!' said Bunyon. 'If you ever decide to give up being an engineer, Mr Jones, I'm sure there'd be a place for you in the detective branch of the police force!' What he didn't add out loud, but was certainly thinking, was, *if you didn't spit so much.*

When the detective inspector showed the piece of gold brocade to various members of the household, Mad Uncle Jack recognised it at once.

'That's off Private No-Sir's uniform!' he said.

'Private No-Sir, sir?' asked the detective inspector.

'One of my men.'

'Men?'

'One of the four ex-soldiers in my old regiment who now work for me.'

'Aha,' nodded the inspector. 'One of them. Is his name really No-Sir?'

'No.'

'No?'

Mad Uncle Jack shook his head, his beakie nose cutting through the air like a wire cutter through cheese. 'I can't remember his real name. Called him No-Sir for so long.'

'And why do you call him that?'

'Damned if I can remember!' snorted MUJ.

Only seven people under Mad Uncle Jack survived from his entire regiment, after whatever the final campaign it was that they fought in. It wasn't the biggest of regiments, but that was still a pitifully small number. Soon after, two men died (one in an accident and the other of an extremely rare disease contracted from sponging down cacti in a private botanical garden near Norwich). This left five men, all of whom were in the 'lower ranks' and all of whom chose to go and work for Mad Major Jack Dickens at Awful End. Since then, one (a certain Private Gorey) had died not so very long before the events related in this book. Then there were four.

Private No-Sir's real name was Private Norman Sorrel, but the joke in his ever-decreasing regiment was that his initials, N.S., actually stood for 'No Sir' because he was always refusing to carry out orders. This is probably what saved his life. Officers even more senior that MUJ were forever sending men on terribly dangerous missions from which it was unlikely they'd ever return . . . except, perhaps in small pieces. MUJ, meanwhile, was forever making equally dangerous demands of them, but in a more low key manner. Instead of ordering them to 'capture an enemy position' or 'hold the line' (whatever that may mean), he was asking them to try to catch cannon balls, or to nip across to the enemy encampment to ask them to keep the noise down.

Private Sorrel should probably have been court-martialled for insubordination in the ranks, or some such thing. Instead, he ended up with the nickname Private No-Sir, ignored all crazy orders – though he was always happy to retreat when told to – and came out of the various conflicts in one piece.

What's interesting is that those five survivors remained very loyal to MUJ and were happy to work for him at Awful End. This was, no doubt, partly to do with the fact that he appeared to know no fear.

Having never had it explained to him that being hit by a cannon ball or a mortar shell or a bullet might not only hurt him but also do some serious damage or even, believe it or not, kill him, Mad Major Jack Dickens pottered about various battlefields as though he was surveying his vegetable patch. He thought nothing of strolling through enemy fire to inspect a particularly interesting specimen of insect, or to heave a wounded soldier on to his back and carry him off to a hospital tent with little more than a 'And what have you managed to do to yourself this time?'.

Occasionally he would have lucid moments where he seemed to realise that there were nasty foreigners trying to make life difficult for him; or that a particular bridge, or building or piece of land needed defending, but much of the time was spent asking people not to point that thing at him.

Detective Inspector Bunyon rubbed the gold brocade between his fingers. 'And why does Ex-Private No-Sir still go around in uniform?' he asked.

'I've never really thought about it,' said MUJ. 'He always does, that's all. Perhaps he doesn't own any other clothes. Come to think of it, all four of them pong a bit . . .'

'Couldn't you insist that they spend some of their wages on new clothing?' the inspector suggested.

'Wages?' asked Mad Uncle Jack, as though the word was new to him.

The policeman steered the conversation back on track. 'You suspect that this comes from No-Sir's uniform because he's the only one who still wears a uniform?'

MUJ nodded. 'Of course, Gorey used to as well.'

'Gorey used to as well?'

'That's what I said.'

'And who's Gorey, sir?'

'He's a very ex ex-private,' sighed Eddie's great-uncle. 'Sadly no more.'

The detective inspector asked to see No-Sir and they found him with the others playing cards on an iron girder. (All work had stopped on the bridge following the accident that increasingly looked like it hadn't been an accident.) Mad Uncle Jack asked him to step to one side.

Sure enough, No-Sir was in uniform – albeit a very tatty, worn and faded one – and even had a row of four medals. One, battered and bent, read 'BEST OF BREED' and had originally belonged to Gorey. Another was a campaign medal. The third read 'I'VE BEEN TO BLACKPOOL' and the fourth, on closer inspection, appeared not to be a medal at all but a flattened bottle top.

Detective Inspector Bunyon looked at No-Sir's epaulettes (or what was left of them) and at the piece of brocade in his hand. It would have been clear even to the untrained eye that the material came from the ex-private's left shoulder.

'Perhaps you'd like to explain what you were doing on the roof,' said the policeman.

'When, sir?' asked the ex-soldier.

'When what?' asked the detective inspector.

'What was I doing on the roof *when*?' asked No-Sir.

'You mean to tell me that you regularly go up onto the roof?' asked Bunyon. 'Why?'

Ex-Private Norman No-Sir Sorrel nodded his head in the direction of his ex-commanding officer.

The detective inspector took the hint. He was a good detective inspector. He turned to Mad Uncle Jack. 'I think I'd better talk to this man alone, sir,' he said.

'Very well,' said MUJ, who was rapidly losing interest anyway. 'I shall stride purposefully in this direction!'

The two men watched him go. Detective Inspector Bunyon turned back to Sorrel. 'Why do you go up to the roof sometimes?' he asked.

'To hide,' said No-Sir.

'To hide?'

'Yes, sir.'

'From whom?' asked the inspector.

'From Mad Major Dickens . . . from Even Madder Mrs Dickens . . . their nephew, Mr Dickens . . . his nephew's wife . . .'

'Basically, the entire Dickens family?' asked Bunyon.

'Except for Master Edmund,' said the ex-soldier, referring, of course, to Eddie. 'He seems . . .'

There was a pause. 'Normal?' the policeman suggested.

'That's it, sir,' nodded No-Sir. 'The very word I was looking for.'

'But why hide?'

'They're always wanting us to do things and I don't always want to.'

'And saying "no, sir," doesn't always work?'

'No, sir.'

'And when were you last up on the roof?'

'When Mad Major Dickens wanted us to beat the bounds,' said No-Sir.

'And you had nothing to do with dropping the chimney over the edge?' asked Bunyon.

'Oh, no, sir! I'd never do nothing like that.'

'So you know nothing about it?'

The old soldier looked at the detective inspector long and hard. 'I didn't say that,' he said.

Two Neds

*In which some bright spark could point out
that two Neds are better than one*

Baby Ned cried all the way back to Lamberley Monastery. Brother Guck only stopped once in his journey, and that was to stick moss in his ears. It didn't do much to block out the sound, but it looked nice.

Brother Guck tried singing. (He was good at chanting.) He tried a few monkish jokes. He tried everything he could think of, but Ned just cried and cried and cried.

Back at the monastery, Abbot Po didn't fare any better. His soothing voice which, given half the chance, could probably have convinced man-eating tigers to become vegetarian, had no effect whatsoever. Ned simply went on crying.

He only stopped crying when Eddie came to the abbot's office to find out what the noise was about. Eddie looked at Ned. Ned looked at Eddie. And smiled. And gurgled. And *coooooed*.

'Neddie, meet Ned,' said the abbot. 'Though I'm still not absolutely clear how he comes to be with us, I think from what Brother Guck here, said, Baby Ned is another lost soul.'

Brother Guck was watching the way the two boys were looking at each other.

'Do you know this baby, Neddie?' he asked.

'He does look familiar,' said Eddie, trying to fight his way through the fog of amnesia. It was no use.

'He was found by the family living over at Awful End,' said the monk.

'Awful End?' said Eddie. The name meant nothing to him.

'It's the biggest house around here after Lamberley Hall,' said Abbot Po.

(Lamberley Hall has since been converted into 'luxury apartments' which, in this instance, is a posh phrase for lots of badly-converted flats. It's almost entirely populated by people who like to crunch up the swish driveway imagining that they own the whole house, when they really live in a few awkwardly-shaped rooms and pay a huge annual service fee for someone to mow all the lawns and put over-the-top bouquets of flowers on the big round table in the centre of the communal hall.)

'Awful End is a strange name for a house,' said Eddie.

'And a strange family lives there!' said Brother Guck. And maybe if he'd had a chance to describe a few of what were, unbeknownst to all three of them, Eddie's closest relatives, something might have jogged Eddie's befuddled mind.

As it was, Abbot Po interrupted. 'It's not for us to judge who is strange and who is not. Our behaviour may seem strange to some outsiders.'

'You mean the scratchy habits, the humorous undergarments and the nearly-but-not-quite cutting yourself off from everyone?'

Po nodded. 'That and our belief in God,' he added.

Eddie was now holding Baby Ned. There was something familiar about him. The freshly powdered baby smell, perhaps?

'Until I decide what we can do about the child, perhaps you'd be kind enough to look after him, Neddie?' the abbot asked Eddie. 'Know you or not, he's certainly taken a shine to you.'

'I'd be happy to,' said Eddie.

★

The detective inspector was staring at No-Sir. 'You're claiming that you saw *Master Edmund* push the chimney on to his father?' he asked, struggling to control his professional composure.

'That's exactly what I'm claiming. Yes, sir,' said No-Sir, who had, indeed, made the startling revelation only moments before.

'What about all the eyewitnesses who state that he was right next to his father, down on the driveway, when the chimney flattened him?'

'So you don't believe me, then, sir?' said No-Sir.

'I don't believe you then.'

'Are you calling me a liar?'

'I'm suggesting that you were mistaken, at the very least,' said the detective.

'Like I said, the chimney was already balanced sideways on the parapet when I came out onto the roof and, moments later, I saw Master Edmund give it a shove.'

'And you're sure it was him?'

'As sure as eggs is eggs.'

'As eggs is eggs?' asked the detective inspector.

'As eggs is eggs,' No-Sir nodded.

'Which leaves me with four possibilities. One, you are lying –' The ex-soldier was about to protest, but Inspector Bunyon frowned. Despite looking like a stick insect in comedy clown pants, he still had that indefinable air of authority about him, and No-Sir fell silent. 'Two, you imagined the whole thing. Three, you are mistaken. You genuinely thought you saw Edmund Dickens but, in actuality, you did not.'

'And four?' asked No-Sir.

'I was just coming to that,' said the inspector, 'and four, you were right – it *was* Master Edmund – and everyone else was mistaken.'

'It must be that last one,' said No-Sir, emphatically.

'I'm inclined to give you the benefit of the doubt at this stage,' said the policeman, 'and am willing to rule out options one and, possibly, even option two. You don't drink, do you?'

'Oh, yes, sir!' said No-Sir proudly. 'Gallons of the stuff. That's what they teaches you to do in the army.'

Detective Inspector Bunyon had a fleeting image of men being given their daily grog ration, then decided that that was for sailors in Her Majesty's Navy.

'Stops deforestation,' No-Sir explained.

The inspector looked at him like he was an idiot, which was probably appropriate. 'Do you mean dehydration?' he asked.

'That too,' said No-Sir, his medals jangling.

'So when you say that you drink, you mean water, don't you?'

'The very same, sir,' said the ex-private. 'Adam's Ale.'

'We all drink, man!' said the inspector. 'If we didn't drink, we'd die!'

'My point exactly, sir,' said No-Sir. 'Which is what they teaches us in the army.'

'So when I asked whether you drink, I meant *drink* drink, not drink . . . Don't you see?' asked the now somewhat exasperated policeman.

'No, sir,' said No-Sir.

'Do you drink alcohol?'

'Never touch the stuff.'

'Never?'

'No, sir,' said No-Sir.

'Good,' said the detective inspector. 'Then I'm inclined to rule out the first two options, which leaves three and four. And your being mistaken, rather than everyone else, seems likelier, doesn't it?

Detective Inspector Humphrey Bunyon had steered Ex-Private Sorrel away from his three card-playing companions and they were now some way off. From their vantage point on the lawn, he looked back at the iron skeleton of the tree-house and Fandango Jones's bridge that was beginning to take shape.

'What is the point of this bridge you're building?' he asked the old soldier.

'None whatsoever, sir,' he replied. 'It's a mad idea. Not as dangerous as some of the things we're asked to do, though, and I quite enjoys the riveting.'

'So nothing the Dickenses get up to surprises you any more?'

'Not really, sir,' said No-Sir.

'So Master Edmund pushing that chimney over the edge was just another typical Dickens act then, was it?'

'Yes and no, sir,' said No-Sir.

'Yes *and* no?'

'Yes it would have been another typical Dickens act if it had been any Dickens but Master Edmund doing it.'

'But Master Edmund is – what did you call him? – normal. And dropping a chimney on to one's family is hardly normal, now, is it?'

'That's my point exactly, sir,' said No-Sir. 'Though I can't blame him.'

'*You can't blame him*?'

'There's many a time I've wanted to strangle Mad Major Dickens, or run him over with a train, or poison him, or stab him repeatedly –'

'Repeatedly?'

'It means again and again, inspector.'

'I know what it means,' said Bunyon, 'I was simply wondering why you wanted to do these things, and why you're confessing them to a police officer?'

'Oh, you'd want to do the same if you worked here for any length of time, sir,' said No-Sir, with utter conviction. 'We all of us feels this way. They're quite mad, you see . . . Forever changing their minds and wanting the most ridiculous things done.'

'For example?' asked Bunyon.

'Like the time Even Madder Mrs Dickens made Private Drabb stand atop of me, then painted black rings around us at one-foot intervals.'

'Why on earth did she do that?'

'That's what I was wondering at the time. I should have guessed when she insisted on *waterproof* paint.'

'Because?' asked the detective.

'Because she then made us wade into the middle of that there lake,' said No-Sir. 'She were using us to see how deep it was.'

'A human depth gauge!'

'Exactly, sir. A measuring rod. Only we was no good at it because the water was deeper than we were tall.'

'I can appreciate that life here at Awful End might be a little – er – frustrating at times,' said the detective inspector, 'but I do hope that you never resort to physical violence.'

'Oh, no-sir!' said No-Sir, snapping to attention as best a man of his age and health could snap to attention. (There was, in fact, an actual snapping noise as he did so. Bunyon hoped that it wasn't the poor man's bones.) 'We all thinks it, but we'd never do nothing about it, see?'

'I see.'

'Thank you, Private Sorrel. You've been most helpful,' said the inspector. 'Now I'm going to have another look at that roof. In the meantime, my men must start the search for this missing Master Edmund.'

You see. No one mentioned Baby Ned. Not one of them. During Detective Inspector Humphrey Bunyon's brief visit to Awful End (long before Brother Guck came to call, of course), Gibbering

Jane happened to be taking Ned for a walk around the grounds in his pram, which is short for perambulator, from the verb to perambulate, from the Latin *perambulare*, meaning to walk about. Interestingly (or not, as the case may be), in its British historical sense, perambulate meant to walk around in order to assert and record a place's boundaries . . . which is a bit like beating the bounds back in chapter whatever.

Even *more* interestingly (or not, *see above*), baby Ned's pram and/or perambulator was a somewhat makeshift, home-made affair. The main body of the pram was another of the old dresser drawers, and the four wheels were made from cross-sections of a large log that Eddie's father, Mr Dickens, had made MUJ's ex-soldiers cut up in order for him to carve from. (I suspect that lump of old wood, next to the chunk of stone, in the broom cupboard that MUJ and EMAM mistook for the private chapel, had something to do with Mr Dickens's attempt at carving, too.)

Anyway, the pram-of-sorts was proudly made for Baby Ned by Dawkins at Gibbering Jane's request. Of course, Gibbering Jane's request had included much gibbering – one would expect no less from her – so it had taken time for the gentleman's gentleman to make head or tail of what she was saying. In fact, he had enough time to rustle up an eggy snack for himself and Jane whilst she was trying to make herself understood. It was whilst he was washing up the frying pan that everything fell into place and he realised that a pram was required of him.

Lacking any suspension, the end result – of the pram-making, not the pan-washing – was a bit of a boneshaker, but Ned seemed to love it. He spent much time laughing as he was wheeled judderingly about the place. He seemed blissfully happy if Eddie or Jane was with him and, with Eddie currently out of the picture, Gibbering Jane was doing a grand job.

Gibbering Jane's favourite walk with Ned was along the edge of Awful Wood. Awful Wood existed long before Awful End although it was now a part of the house's grounds (and still is today). I suspect the house must have got its name from the wood, or *gotten* its name from the *woods* if you're American.

If you're wondering why anyone would name a wood 'awful', especially when it wasn't that bad, I suppose it's my duty to point out that although 'awful' has come to mean bad or unpleasant, it also used to mean 'to fill one with awe'. For those of you who only know 'awe' as the noise the movie star John Wayne used to make when he drawled, let me tell you that it also means a feeling of reverential respect mixed with wonder or, sometimes, fear. So far from being a grotty wood, this was once seen as being pretty amazing.

Walking past it now, wheeling Baby Ned in front of her, gibbering away happily to him, Gibbering Jane caught a glimpse of what looked to her like a Red Indian wigwam nestling between the trees, but which could be more accurately described as a Native American-style tepee (what with Native Americans being neither red nor from India, and the thing Jane saw being tent-like, and a wigwam being more dome-shaped).

When Gibbering Jane finally returned to the house, the police had long gone and all the talk was of attempted murder, Eddie and Horsey's disappearance and what to have for supper. Baby Ned couldn't have been further from their minds.

Episode 10

'Here's Eddie!'

In which saying too much here
might give the game away

The fact that the monks at Lamberley Monastery didn't take baby Ned straight to the police made Eddie think about his own situation. Obviously, his primary concern had been to try to get his memory back, and the monks had been very kind to him. Because he didn't know who he was or where he rightfully belonged, he wasn't missing anywhere specific and, anyway, he liked it there. This had meant that, strange though he found some of the rules the Bertian order had about getting involved-but-only-so-far in the outside world, he hadn't been too bothered by them.

In the past few days, however, Eddie was beginning to think that he should visit the police station himself. There was nothing to stop him going out and about, and he should probably take Ned with him.

Eddie decided to speak to Abbot Po about it. As usual, he found him in his office.

'I've decided to go into town,' said Eddie.

'You're leaving us?' asked the abbot.

'No . . . I was thinking more of a day trip,' said Eddie. 'I'd like to carry on living here with you until I'm claimed.' He paused. 'If that's all right?'

Abbot Po looked at Eddie across his big oak desk. 'Of course you can stay with us, Neddie, for as long as you like.'

'Thank you,' said Eddie. 'I wasn't sure you'd say yes.'

Abbot Po looked at his hands. 'I've been waiting for you to ask to visit the town,' he said. 'I knew that you'd come around to it in your own good time, and that would prove you were ready to make the next step. This had to be a decision you came to yourself.'

'I'd like to take Ned with me,' Eddie suggested. 'His parents may be worried.'

'It would probably be better to leave him here for the time being,' said Po. 'He's getting better treatment than he'd get from any nurse or certainly any poor-house or orphanage. But, by all means, tell the authorities of his whereabouts.'

'That's a great idea,' said Eddie.

'As a matter of fact, we have a lad of about your own age visiting the monastery today,' said Po, getting to his feet. 'He's interested in the possibility of taking up religious orders so his father made arrangements for him to come and see us. When he's finished, I'll ask him to accompany you into town. It's a big step you're taking, Neddie. It'd be good for you to have young company.'

'Thank you,' said Eddie, blissfully unaware that things were about to change in a big way.

He spent the rest of the morning helping some of the brothers make a more permanent repair to the break in the fence that had allowed the sheep to escape. It was whilst he was being chased around the field by one of the friskier of the fleecy beasts that he had another one of his flashbacks. This time he had memories of being chased by policemen with sheep on leashes . . . if they *were* memories. It seemed far more likely that his befuddled mind was playing tricks on him again. All these so-called flashbacks he'd had were so *weird*.

A job well done, Eddie, Brother Guck, Brother Pugh and a Brother Klaus were sitting under a tree, sharing a pitcher of water. (That's a pitcher as in jug, rather than something you look at hanging on the wall of a gallery.) Brother Po came striding across the pasture with a boy at his side.

David Thackery, for it was he (and if you can't remember who this particular *he* was, look back at page 33 to refresh your sadly-failing memory), was surprised to find Eddie Dickens in a monastery of all places *and* dressed in a habit. The truth be told, he was a little jealous. 'Eddie!' he said.

'Neddie,' Eddie corrected him, because he'd got so used to this being his name.

'No, David,' said David, thinking that Eddie thought that *he* was someone called Neddie, rather than Eddie telling him that his own name was Neddie which, of course, it wasn't anyway. (You get the idea.)

'My name's really David?' asked Eddie in amazement.

'It's Eddie, stupid!' said David impatiently. 'What is this? Some sort of a game?'

'Wait a minute! Wait a minute!' said Abbot Po. 'Are you telling me that you *know* this young man?'

'I most certainly do, abbot,' said the Thackery boy. 'Has he been playing tricks on you?'

'Please answer the question, child,' said Po. 'Do you know who this boy is?'

'He's Edmund Dickens from Awful End,' said David Thackery.

'Awful End!' gasped Brother Guck. 'I was there only the other day.'

'Do you recognise David Thackery?' Abbot Po asked Eddie, who'd leapt to his feet. He put a hand on the shoulder of each boy.

Eddie shook his head.

'And the name Edmund Dickens – Eddie – doesn't mean anything to you?'

Eddie shook his head again.

Abbot Po turned to David Thackery. 'You're in absolutely no doubt that this is Eddie Dickens?'

'None whatsoever, sir,' said David. 'I promise you, that's who he is.' And David wouldn't break a promise. He wanted to be a saint one day, remember? 'His parents and my parents are best friends.'

'Eddie,' said Abbot Po. 'This is the lad I was telling you about. The one who's interested in taking up religious orders. God certainly works in mysterious ways!'

Now any half-decent storyteller would have put the conversation Eddie and the abbot had regarding the up-coming visit from the (then) unnamed boy much, much earlier in the story. That way, when David turned up, the reader would go, 'Oh, so *that's* who it was!' having pretty much forgotten that anyone was due to turn up at all.

This way (*my* way), one minute you're told the boy's due to come and BAM! – a few paragraphs later – here he is and he turns out to be David Thackery. Not much of a build-up there, is there? No evidence of multi-layered storytelling or planting the seed of an idea. No suspense. No. But, then again, that's how it happened, so that's how I'm telling it. Publish the Truth with a capital 'T' and be damned, I say!

And where does this leave us? With Abbot Po and Brother Guck taking Eddie back to Awful End.

*

And here we are:

It was Even Madder Aunt Maud who opened the door to them.

'Do you know this boy, madam?' asked the Abbot, eager to get straight to the point.

'I've never seen him before in my life,' said EMAM.

'You're sure?'

Even Madder Aunt Maud leaned in closer and peered at them all in more detail. 'I tell a lie,' she said. 'He came here the other day asking about sheep, and took away young Ned with him,' she said.

'That's Brother Guck –'

'A ridiculous name, if ever I heard one,' said Eddie's great-aunt.

'I was referring to this boy, here,' said Po, putting his hands on Eddie's shoulders and pushing him forward, his heels skidding on the gravel. The abbot was beginning to suspect that this woman might be a little *unusual*.

'Oh, *him*,' said Even Madder Aunt Maud. 'Of course I know *him*. He's my missing great-nephew, Edmund. Why ask me if I know my own great-nephew?'

'He doesn't know he's your great-nephew, you see,' said the abbot.

'Does that mean I don't have to buy him Christmas or birthday presents any more?' she asked, obviously keen on the idea.

'Well, he's missing no more, madam,' said Abbot Po. 'It's my happy duty to return him to you.'

'So you've found him then?'

'He's standing right in front of you.'

'So he is,' said EMAM, adding a 'silly me' with a fluttering-of-the-eyelashes that only her beloved husband Jack would find endearing. To anyone else, it was about as appealing as being in an ascending room/lift/elevator with a flatulent hippo. 'Why's he dressed in a sack?'

'It's a habit,' the abbot explained.

'Well, it's a very silly habit, if you ask me, and one he should grow out of,' snapped Even Madder Aunt Maud.

'Are you really my great-aunt, madam?' Eddie asked politely. The truth be told, there was something more than a little terrifying at the prospect of having this . . . this *lady* as a relative.

'Well, I'm hardly a tucker bag full of jumbucks, now, am I?' she demanded, proud to be able to employ some everyday Australian speech that she'd gleaned from a book entitled *Everyday Australian Speech*.

'Indeed not, no,' said Eddie, beginning to wonder whether life in a monastery wouldn't be such a bad option after all.

'Are the boy's parents at home?' asked Abbot Po. David Thackery had mentioned his mother and father being friends of Eddie's parents.

'Mr Dickens is currently indisposed, a chimney

124

having been pushed upon him,' said Eddie's great-aunt, unable to suppress a chuckle. 'I'm a great believer in seeing the funny side of things.'

'Not so funny for my father, I suppose,' said Eddie.

'You're behaving very oddly, boy,' said EMAM, fixing a stare on Eddie.

'The child has lost his memory,' the abbot said. 'If we might be allowed in to see his parents – his mother, at least – I can explain everything.'

'No memory, you say?'

'Not of his family, no, madam.'

'Ridiculous!'

'Helping him regain it could be a slow process,' said Abbot Po. 'The mind is a delicate tool and –' He was interrupted by a loud 'THUMP!'

The loud 'THUMP!' was generated by Even Madder Aunt Maud leaning back inside the doorway, lifting Malcolm the stuffed stoat from an occasional table just out of view, and hitting Eddie over the head with him.

Slightly dazed, Eddie blinked, then looked from Malcolm to Even Madder Aunt Maud and back to Malcolm. Suddenly, the world made *sense* again.

'Malcolm!' he said in delight, throwing his arms around the rigid animal. 'Now I remember everything!'

'Cured!' said his great-aunt triumphantly. 'Now there's no time to stand around talking, I need to get on!'

She slammed the front door, leaving Abbot Po, Brother Guck and Eddie out on the driveway.

'That's Even Madder Aunt Maud,' said Eddie.

'Delighted to meet her,' said Abbot Po.

'My great-aunt,' said Eddie.

'Charmed, I'm sure,' said Po.

The front door flew back open. 'And might I just add that you're the ugliest man I've ever seen,' said Maud, before slamming it shut again.

None of them had to guess who she was talking to, or even to whom she was talking.

There was much back-slapping and a few tears when Eddie was welcomed back into the bosom of his family. Gibbering Jane had been so upset when Even Madder Aunt Maud had given Baby Ned to Brother Guck that she'd gone back to the cupboard under the stairs and refused to come out. Now that Eddie was back, she emerged. Eddie was quick to assure her that little Ned was safe and well – and bawling his eyes out – back at Lamberley Monastery. She gibbered with delight at the news.

Mad Uncle Jack shook Eddie's hand solemnly. 'I take it that you told the enemy nothing?' he asked.

'I was in an accident,' Eddie explained for the umpteenth time. 'I lost my memory.'

'So that's what you told the blackguards, huh? And they believed you? Excellent, my boy! I knew that a Dickens would never talk under interrogation. We're part of what makes this country great: chin up . . . stiff upper lip . . . eyes front, and all that!'

In Eddie's absence, his mother (Mrs Dickens, of course) had 'knitted' him a suit using the unravelled material from the sofa. 'It was my way of telling myself that you'd be back,' she said, kissing her son on the forehead. Her breath smelled of mothballs. She'd been sucking on a handful now and then, to calm the nerves.

Eddie changed out of his monk's habit and into the suit. Looking at himself in the wardrobe mirror, he quickly changed back again.

Mr Dickens was delighted to see Eddie, but could still only manage a horizontal position. He'd solved this by asking his wife – Mrs Dickens to you and me – to lash him to the tea trolley he remembered from his youth. Mrs Dickens hadn't been able to find any rope at such short notice (or of such a short length) so had used some bunting last hung out for one of the Queen's jubilees.

It was in this extraordinary state that his father first greeted Eddie on his return. It'd be interesting to know what Eddie would have made of this if he'd met his father in this condition *before* his memory came back to him. As it was, this was just another typical Dickens family scene.

'Fandango Jones – you remember him, I take it?' asked Mr Dickens. Eddie nodded. 'He had a theory that the chimney was deliberately pushed from the roof; a theory which the detective inspector –'

'The same detective inspector?' asked Eddie.

'The very same,' nodded his father, with a wince. 'The fat one with the checked suit. Only now he's very thin, but still has the same suit. Well, he agrees with Jones. He says that this was no accident, not that I was necessarily the target.'

'How dreadful!' said Eddie.

'Nothing a piece of sacking wouldn't fix,' said Even Madder Aunt Maud, passing by with what appeared to be a stuffed moose's head (mounted on a wooden shield) under her arm.

'I beg your pardon?' asked Eddie.

'I assume you were referring to the abbot's ugliness. I was saying it's nothing a piece of sacking wouldn't fix! He could cut out a pair of holes for his eyes.'

'He was referring to someone deliberately pushing that chimney on to me,' said Eddie's father, somewhat indignantly. 'And where are you going with that moose head?'

'What moose head?' asked his aunt.

'*That* moose head,' Mr Dickens managed to point. 'Under your arm.'

EMAM looked down and flinched in surprise as though noticing the moose head for the first time. 'I read somewhere that they make nourishing soup,' she said, somewhat unconvincingly. I'd hazard a guess that she had no idea why she was carrying it either.

'I think she's thinking of carrots,' muttered Laudanum Dickens as she strode out of earshot.

Eddie found that he couldn't sleep that first night back at Awful End. It was a strange feeling getting all his memories back, even though they were rightfully his. It wasn't so much the having-regained-his-identity part that was so odd but the looking-back-at-his-time-in-the-monastery now that he knew who he was. It was difficult to remember what it was like *not* knowing. And if you find my trying to explain that confusing, think how hard it was for Eddie to make sense of it in his head.

After staring at the ceiling for what seemed like an eternity, Eddie got up and went for a wander around the house, to try to stop his brain working overtime. It was a moonlit night and Awful End had more than its fair share of curtainless windows, especially since, some years previously, Mad Uncle Jack had used so many of the curtains to fuel an enormous beacon to warn of the coming of the Armada. (Of course, he'd been confused.

130

He'd read in his newspaper a report marking the *anniversary* of the coming of the Spanish fleet some three hundred years earlier but had mistaken it for current news.) Still, the local fire brigade – also known as three men and a horse-drawn fire cart – had great fun trying to douse the flames, and the only victims were the local ducks who were homeless because the fire fighters had drawn all the water for their hoses from their pond. The Thackery family (with the notable exception of Master David, of course) had rallied around, travelling up especially, and giving the ducks temporary accommodation whilst their original watery home was restored to its former glory.

Eddie decided to go up on to the roof. He liked doing that some summer evenings. It was usually a haven of peace and quiet in an otherwise frenetic household. Away from the big windows, the enclosed upper stairways were in darkness. Eddie held up his bedside candle before him.

Out on the roof, he placed the candle on the parapet. The air was so still that the flame barely flickered. Eddie looked up at the star-filled night sky, dark blue in the moonlight. Then something caught his eye.

There, over in Awful Wood, was a glimmering light. Someone had lit a camp-fire on the estate. Eddie was too far away to make out anything

131

more. Had he been closer, he would have seen the strange tent that Gibbering Jane had passed that day of her afternoon perambulations with Baby Ned. Of course, she'd failed to mention it to anyone or, if she had, they'd probably failed to understand her through all that gibbering.

Eddie wasn't too alarmed by the sight. It was clearly a self-contained camp-fire and not a danger to property. He guessed that it must be one of his great-uncle's ex-soldiers practising night manoeuvres, or some such thing. He yawned. He'd investigate in the morning.

Falling Into Place

*In which Eddie Dickens makes
a startling discovery and a late breakfast*

To English ears and eyes – well, to mine, at least – the word doppelganger doesn't sound like it means anything, and looks made-up. But, no! Apparently, it's from the German meaning 'double-goer'. Double-goer? Well, a doppelganger is your double. If you come face-to-face with yourself in the high street, then that person is your doppelganger, or you're theirs . . . or both. Unless, of course, you're looking at your own reflection in a shop window, or anywhere else for that matter.

Eddie met his doppelganger when he'd made his way across the lawns and into Awful Wood, the following morning. He saw the tent before he saw the remains of the fire, now long since turned to ashes, that had caught his attention the previous night. The tent was expertly constructed from branches and leaves collected from the wood.

'Is there anyone in there?' he asked, not knowing who to expect. Life at Awful End was full of surprises and, for all Eddie knew, Even Madder Aunt Maud had hired a dwarf to pretend to be a garden ornament by day and live in the wood at night. He wouldn't put it past her.

What he didn't expect was the person who came blinking into the morning sunlight to look how he looked. Eddie blinked. Twice. And then again, for good measure.

He and the boy-emerging-from-the-tent looked remarkably like each other. *Like two peas in a pod.*

The boy-who-had-now-emerged-from-his-tent looked equally startled.

'Good morning,' said Eddie, politely. 'I don't think we've met.'

'No,' said the boy. 'I don't think we have.'

They even sounded similar. The boy was a fraction taller than Eddie and his hair was a lighter shade of brown.

'You're Fabian, aren't you?' said Eddie. 'Hester's boy.'

Fabian, for that was, indeed, who he was, was flabbergasted (and what a brilliant word that is).

134

'How . . . how on earth did you know that?' asked Fabian. He furtively looked from left to right, as though he was expecting that this was some kind of trap, and that a swarm of peelers might appear from behind the trees and start beating him with their truncheons.

Of course, the reason that Eddie knew that Fabian was Fabian was because he guessed that there couldn't be that many gypsies of about his age and appearance loose in the countryside; and there was no doubting that Fabian was a gypsy, what with the clothes he was wearing and the skills with which he'd made the tent from branches in the wood.

'I keep my ears open,' Eddie grinned. 'And Chief Fudd is out looking for you.'

'Has he been to the house?' asked Fabian, nodding in the direction of Awful End.

Eddie shrugged. 'I've been away,' he said, 'but no one here's mentioned him to me.'

Fabian took a knife out of his pocket and began to whittle a small piece of wood which he took from the other. Eddie was tinged with jealousy. His parents only let him whittle with a carrot, which is another way of saying 'not at all', carrots being one of the blunter vegetables. Whittling was out for Eddie. They were worried he might cut himself. Eddie was pretty sure – which is similar to fairly confident – that Fabian had primarily produced the knife not to whittle but to let Eddie know that he was armed. It was obvious from his manner that he was jumpy about something. He looked decidedly uneasy.

'You went off the day that the chimney landed on that man,' said Fabian.

'That's right,' said Eddie. 'The man is my father. I went to fetch the doctor.'

'Is he all right? Your father, I mean,' asked the gypsy boy.

'He's always having accidents,' said Eddie. 'The doctor says that he'll make a full recovery.'

'That's good,' said Fabian. 'What happened to you? You didn't come back.'

'Until now,' said Eddie. 'I was waylaid.'

There was a period of silence between them. Fabian whittled and Eddie stuck his hands in his pockets.

'Is this a bad place?' asked Fabian, when he next spoke.

'Bad?' said Eddie, in genuine surprise. 'Mad, maybe, but I wouldn't say bad.'

'What about the beatings?' asked Fabian.

'Beatings?' asked Eddie. The only beating he could think of was being beaten over the head with Malcolm, and that had done him the power of good.

'The day you went and didn't come back. The tall beaky man was talking about beating people . . .'

'Oh,' said Eddie. 'You mean beating the bounds! He was only going to hit a well-padded ex-soldier with a stuffed stoat.' The minute the words came out, he realised how odd they'd sound to a stranger. But just how much of a stranger could someone who looked so like Eddie be?

'And what about Oli– about the baby?' asked Fabian. 'What happened to the baby? They let someone take him away!'

'You seem to know an awful lot about what's been going on here,' said Eddie. 'Who exactly are you?'

There was the loud flap of a wood pigeon's wings as it took flight, and Fabian threw himself to the ground as though dodging a bullet.

Eddie put his hand out, which Fabian sheepishly took, pulling himself back to his feet. He stuffed the knife and whittled wood back into a pocket.

'Are you a relation?' Eddie asked.

'A relation?'

'Are you and I related in some way?' asked Eddie. 'You must have noticed how similar we look.'

'I – er –' Fabian stuttered to a halt. 'The baby?'

'The baby's fine. He hasn't been stuck in any poor-house or orphanage. He's staying with some monks for the time being.' Just at that moment, Fabian's tummy rumbled and Eddie seized the opportunity to turn the situation to his advantage. 'Do you want to come up to the house for something to eat? We've had our breakfast, but there's always plenty left over.'

Fabian seemed hesitant. 'I – er – I'm not sure I want the others to see me,' he said at last.

'I'm not sure you wanted *me* to see you,' said Eddie. 'It's probably too late now.'

'So they're not bad people?' asked the gypsy boy.

Eddie put his hands on his hips. 'How many times am I going to have to say this: they're not bad, just eccentric. That's all. Come on.'

Eddie sneaked Fabian into the kitchen, sat him at the table, and then went into the larder to find him some leftovers. No one had invented the fridge yet, though someone of Eddie's slight acquaintance (a Tobias Belch) had been experimenting with a 'steam-powered ice box' in his laboratories in Bristol. So far, with little success and a few big explosions.

Eddie returned with some bacon, kedgeree (a kind of cold fish curry designed specifically to be eaten in the morning) and something called 'devilled kidneys', which are not kidneys with little horns and fork tails but those cooked with hot seasoning.

'I would offer you bread, but my mother's is an acquired taste,' said Eddie. He didn't bother to tell Fabian about her special recipe which included those troublesome watch springs.

Fabian ate hungrily. 'We *are* related,' he said, after he'd eaten his last mouthful.

'I thought so,' said Eddie. 'How?'

Fabian wiped his mouth on his sleeve. 'Have you heard of a man named Doctor Malcontent Dickens?' he asked.

'Yes,' said Eddie. 'He was my great-grandfather. That "tall beaky man", as you called him, is his only remaining son, Jack. He's my great-uncle.'

'If he's Jack, then you'll know that Malcontent had two other sons –'

'My grandfather, Percy Dickens, and my Great-Uncle George –'

'The one who burnt down the Houses of Parliament,' Fabian nodded. Eddie could sense that he was getting excited.

'But what I don't understand is where you fit

in?' said Eddie. 'Out of Grandpa, Mad Uncle Jack and George, only my grandfather had a child . . . That's my father, Laudanum. And he, of course, had me.'

Fabian pulled a piece of paper from inside his shirt and unfolded it on the table, smoothing it flat with a fist. 'That's not strictly true,' he said. 'Look at this.'

Eddie found himself looking at an incomplete branch of the Dickens family tree. Sure enough, his father, Laudanum, was down there as being married to Florinda, but there was no mention of their having a son, Edmund. What really caught Eddie's eye, though, was what appeared under George's name.

'My Great-Uncle George had a daughter?' he said in amazement. 'No one ever mentioned that before. In fact, I'm sure that Mad Uncle Jack told me that his brother George never married –' It's true, you know. That's exactly what MUJ told Eddie. If you don't believe me, you'll find it on page 49 of the UK edition of *Terrible Times*. '– let alone had a daughter.'

'She's my mother,' said Fabian, producing a stubby pencil from a pocket, and adding the next generation to the family tree.

Here's what it looked like after Fabian had finished with it:

140

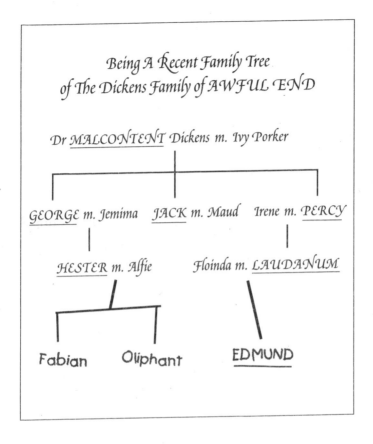

Being A Recent Family Tree
of The Dickens Family of AWFUL END

Dr <u>MALCONTENT</u> Dickens m. Ivy Porker

<u>GEORGE</u> m. Jemima   <u>JACK</u> m. Maud   Irene m. <u>PERCY</u>

<u>HESTER</u> m. Alfie   Floinda m. <u>LAUDANUM</u>

Fabian   Oliphant   <u>EDMUND</u>

'Ned – I mean the baby – is your brother, Oliphant?' gasped Eddie.

'Yes,' said Fabian.

'So it was you who brought him here and put him in amongst the bulrushes!'

'It was my mother's idea,' said Fabian. 'She wants Oliphant to have the life that she never had . . .'

'But what about you?' asked Eddie, pulling out a

chair from under the kitchen table and sitting next to his cousin. 'What about the life *you* never had?'

The story Fabian told was simple enough: 'When my grandfather, your Great-Uncle George, was on a walking tour of the English Channel –'

'But that's the sea!' Eddie protested.

'He had a thing about water,' said Fabian. 'And a big pair of lead boots. He met a boy called Jimmy who was a cook on one of the support vessels.'

'What's a support vessel?' asked Eddie.

'Some kind of large boat or small ship,' said Fabian. 'Can I please tell this?'

'Sorry,' said Eddie.

'Jimmy worked in the galley,' said Fabian (which, from his early years at sea, Eddie knew to be the ship's kitchen). 'Only it turned out that he wasn't a he at all but a she.'

'Jimmy was a girl?'

'A young woman,' said Fabian. 'She couldn't get a job on board ship as a woman, so she disguised herself as a boy. I think this happens quite a lot.'

'Oh,' said Eddie. It was the first he'd heard about it.

'Anyhow,' said his cousin, 'Jimmy – whose real name turned out to be Jemima – and Grandpa George fell in love and, after a whirlwind romance, got married.'

'How romantic!' said Eddie.

'But not popular with his father, Doctor Malcontent, and the other Dickenses.'

'They thought that he was marrying beneath his station?' asked Eddie (which, I'm sure I must have explained in some previous book or other, doesn't mean attending a wedding ceremony under Charing Cross, Grand Central or any such railway terminus, but getting hitched to someone of a 'lower class').

Cousin Fabian shook his head. 'It wasn't that,' he said, 'it's just that the Dickenses had a violent and irrational reaction against anyone whose name began with a "J"!'

'But Mad Uncle Jack's name begins with a "J"!' Eddie protested.

'Except for the name Jack,' Fabian added. 'They had nothing against the name Jack.'

Eddie was about to protest that this made no sense at all, when he remembered that this was his own family he was talking about.

'George was always welcome at Awful End and at family gatherings, so long as he neither brought Jemima with him, nor mentioned her name. Fortunately, this wasn't quite as hard on my grandfather as you might imagine, because he was very absent-minded, and often forgot that he was married.'

'So what happened?'

'Sadly, my grandmother, Jemima, died in childbirth, giving birth to my mother Hester. She was brought up by a kind and loving nanny named Nanny Noonan. What's unusual, is that she was actually christened Nanny Noonan. It wasn't just her title,' Fabian explained. 'Grandpa George never even told his brothers that he'd had a child. When my mother grew up, she felt so rejected by the Dickens family and society that she turned her back on them. When a handsome gypsy turned up at the door of Nanny Nanny Noonan's house one day, offering to sharpen her knives and scissors, my mother ran away with him. They married, and me and Oliphant were the result.'

Eddie was bursting to ask a whole series of questions, when they were rather rudely interrupted.

There was the sound of a stoat-carrying great-aunt in tiny black boots stomping across the stone-flagged kitchen floor.

Even Madder Aunt Maud stopped and stared at the pair of them, seated side-by-side at the long, pine table.

'Edmund!' she snapped. 'I suppose you think it's clever pretending to be two of you! Stop it at once!'

Now she too was interrupted, for into the kitchen walked that fairly well-known engineer Fandango Jones beside the once-fat-now-thin Detective Inspector Humphrey Bunyon.

'I was looking for you, Master Edm–' began the policeman, then he saw that Eddie wasn't alone. Next to him sat a look-alike.

Cogs spun in his brain. Lights flashed. Whistles blew. The detective inspector recalled his conversation with No-Sir: the conversation in which the ex-private had sworn he'd witnessed Eddie pushing the barley-sugar chimney over the parapet . . . whilst everyone else had sworn that Eddie had been down below with them.

Now it made sense: two Eddies. And one was an attempted murderer.

Episode 12

A Conclusion of Sorts

*In which things fall into place,
and a rock falls on the floor*

Fabian could spot a policeman a mile off, even one as strange looking as Humphrey Bunyon. He was up and out of his chair before you could say, 'Hello, hello, hello. What's going on here then?', and dashed out of the kitchen door . . . straight into Mrs Dickens who was carrying what appeared to be a small boulder. She dropped it, narrowly missing both their feet – all four of them/two pairs, I'm not implying that they had one foot each – which was fortunate when you see the dent the rock made in the floor, which is still there to this day (but now covered with a swirly-patterned carpet).

The detective inspector seized the opportunity, and Fabian's collar, lifting the boy off the ground. 'I think you've some explaining to do, young man,' he said.

Even Madder Aunt Maud looked from Eddie at the table to Fabian at the door, and then back again. 'So he isn't you?' she demanded.

'No, Aunt Maud,' said Eddie. 'I'm sitting over here . . . and he isn't.'

Even Madder Aunt Maud studied him between half-closed eyes. 'This isn't another one of your tricks, is it?' she demanded. 'Like that time you wore those stilts and tried to frighten me at my bedroom window.'

'Your bedroom doesn't have a window, Aunt Maud,' he sighed, knowing that she'd imagined the whole thing. 'You live in a cow.'

Even Madder Aunt Maud seemed momentarily stumped by this, then added triumphantly: 'But I see you don't deny it!'

'Let me go! Let me go!' shouted Fabian, to which he would probably have added 'I ain't done nuffink' if it weren't for the fact that he'd been so well brought up by his mother Hester Grout, _née_ Dickens. So what he actually said was: 'I haven't done anything!'

'Then why run?' spat Fandango Jones, his stovepipe hat quivering with excitement. This was like living out one of those penny dreadful detective stories he so loved to read.

'Because no one has a good word to say for gypsies!' he protested.

'Gypsum?' cried Even Madder Aunt Maud prodding Mrs Dickens's dropped lump of rock with Malcolm. 'This isn't gypsum. It looks more like granite to me.'

Very sensibly, the detective inspector ignored her. 'Now just exactly who are you, my boy?' he asked Fabian. 'There's no denying you have a remarkably strong resemblance to Master Edmund, except, of course, for having different coloured eyes.' (Trust a policeman to spot something like that. Though, of course, Chief Fudd must have spotted the same thing at the monastery to know, at a glance, that Eddie wasn't Fabian.)

'He's the cousin I never knew I had,' said Eddie. He turned to Mrs Dickens. 'Mother, this is Great-Uncle George's grandson Fabian.'

Mrs Dickens, who was busy trying to pick up the chunk of rock, looked up at Fabian who was now wearing the desk sergeant's brand new shiny pair of handcuffs. 'So you're a Dickens?' she asked.

'My mother was, ma'am, before she married,' said Fabian politely, even stopping struggling.

'Well I never!' said Eddie's mum. 'I never even knew George had a daughter. Welcome to Awful

End!' She seemed oblivious to the fact that the poor boy was in handcuffs and in the clutches of the law (in the guise of a very skinny man in very baggy clothes).

'Thank you,' said Fabian.

'Why are you arresting Fabian?' Eddie demanded. 'What's he supposed to have done? Trespassed in the wood?'

'Oh, much worse than that, Master Edmund,' said Humphrey Bunyon. 'An eye-witness saw this lad push the chimney over the parapet onto your father.'

Eddie was stunned. 'Is that true?' he asked Fabian.

'It was an accident!' Fabian protested.

'It was a premeditated act!' spat Fandango Jones. 'Don't tell me that you accidentally got the chimney from the stack, down the roof, up on to the parapet and over the edge by mistake!'

'I know my rights!' said Fabian to the policeman. 'Stop that man spitting all over me!'

'The chimney fell off the stack and rolled down the roof,' said Mrs Dickens, who had now managed to lift the boulder to waist height. 'No one moved it. Things like that often happen. This house is in constant need of repair.'

'I beg your pardon?' asked the detective inspector.

'And how did the chimney get up on to the parapet and over the edge?' asked Fandango Jones.

With a grunt of exertion, Mrs Dickens was now holding the rock in her arms again, pressed against her stomach. 'I put it on the parapet,' she said. 'What's this all about, anyway?'

'What's this all about?' spluttered the policeman in absolute amazement. 'This is about a police investigation. Were you not aware, madam, that I've spent heaven-knows-how-long trying to get to the bottom of how your husband came to be flattened by a chimney, and you neglected to tell me that it was you who put the chimney on the parapet in the first instance!'

Realising that she wouldn't be able to get on

with her current task uninterrupted, Mrs Dickens dropped the chunk of rock on the kitchen table, sending an uneaten bite of devilled kidney flying through the air. As it neared EMAM, the old lady batted it aside with Malcolm, and it came to rest in the rim of the fairly well-known engineer's stovepipe hat. He didn't notice, and there it remained for the rest of the day until his wife Clarissa spotted it that evening.

As for the table, the damage caused by the rock knocked quite a significant amount off the reserve price when it was auctioned in the 1960s.

'All I knew was that poor Laudanum had been squashed by the chimney and that you two gentlemen,' she was referring to Bunyon and Jones, 'were convinced that it had been dropped. You even told me that you had an eye-witness who saw someone push it over. That certainly wasn't me, so what relevance did anything else have?'

The detective inspector sighed. 'Sit!' he commanded Fabian, who did as he was told and sat back down at the kitchen table. 'Mrs Dickens,' the policeman continued. 'Mr Jones calculated that the chimney could not have fallen from the stack, down the roof and over the edge, something that my later inspection of the scene confirmed. This then led me to suspect that someone had deliberately lifted the chimney on to the parapet with the sole intention of pushing it on to the assembled company below.'

'Us lot below?' asked Even Madder Aunt Maud, who was wondering why Fandango Jones was walking around with a bite-sized piece of devilled kidney in the brim of his extraordinary hat. What was he? Some kind of weirdo?

'You lot below,' nodded the detective inspector. 'Only now you're telling me that it was you who placed the chimney on the parapet in the first instance, Mrs Dickens.'

'Yes,' said Eddie's mother.

'May I ask why?' asked the detective inspector.

'Yes, you may,' said Eddie's mother, rinsing her hands under the kitchen tap.

'Why?' asked the detective inspector, obligingly.

'So that I could push it over the edge.'

'Push it over the edge?'

'Push it over the edge,' said Mrs Dickens. 'That's right.'

'But *why*?'

'Because it was too heavy to carry down all those flights of stairs, inspector. I really don't see where you're going with these questions.'

Detective Inspector Bunyon was doing his very best not to burst into tears. He wanted to be lovely and fat again and as far away from the Dickens family as possible. He hated cases involving the

152

Dickens family. He'd rather be investigating a grizzly murder in a sewer than spending another minute with these infuriating people . . . but he was a good detective inspector, and there was a job to be done.

He tried again. 'Why? Why? Why, Mrs Dickens? *Why* did you want the chimney on the ground when a chimney's rightful place is on a chimney stack? *Why*, once you'd got as far as putting the chimney on the parapet, didn't you then push it? *Why*, Mrs Dickens?' He found it impossible to keep the air of desperation out of his voice.

'You may not be aware of it, inspector, but my husband is a very fine amateur sculptor,' said Mrs Dickens. 'He mainly carves bottle corks and wood, but I've recently suggested that he try stone. He briefly tried carving in coal, but that proved to be a very messy business and also –' she paused to glare at Even Madder Aunt Maud, '– someone, naming no names, kept on eating it.'

'Even better than charcoal biscuits,' EMAM muttered.

'I've been collecting various different types of stone for him to experiment carving with. I got this piece, for example, from the edge of the ornamental lake where Eddie found Ned.'

'Oliphant,' Eddie corrected her, now that he knew the baby's true name.

'Ned?' asked the detective inspector.

'Oliphant?' asked Mrs Dickens.

'Oliphant?' asked the detective inspector.

'The baby,' said Eddie.

'The baby?' asked the inspector. Everyone had still neglected to mention him.

'We found a baby in the bulrushes.'

'Like Ex-Private Moses in the Bible,' said Even Madder Aunt Maud, a trifle confused. (Surprise. Surprise.)

'My brother,' said Fabian. 'I put him there.'

The policeman's brain was beginning to suffer from what, today, we might call information overload. 'We'll come to the baby in a moment,' he said. 'Would someone please get me a glass of water?'

'Certainly,' said Even Madder Aunt Maud. 'Hold this.' She thrust Malcolm into the startled policeman's hands. 'Milk and sugar?'

'J-Just water, please,' he said. He turned back to Mrs Dickens. 'You collected various different types of stone from the house and grounds for your husband to experiment carving with? Is that correct?'

'Exactly, inspector!'

'And you thought that the fallen chimney would be useful for such a purpose?'

'Too true.'

'But, it being so heavy, you decided to heave it up on to the parapet and then push it over on to the driveway, from where you would then collect it and give it to your husband?'

'Oh, yes.'

'But, once you'd got it up on to the parapet, you left it there.' Detective Inspector Bunyon paused. 'Why was that, Mrs Dickens?'

Eddie's mother clearly had to think before replying. 'Oh, I remember!' she said. 'It was about a week before it fell on poor Laudanum. I'd just got the chimney on to the parapet when I spied the postman coming up the drive. I have a cousin in Australia who'd written to say that she was sending me a parcel of books. It was obvious that this was what the man was carrying, so I hurried down to meet him. In the excitement of opening the parcel and sharing the books out amongst the family, I completely forgot about the chimney.'

The detective inspector was finding it hard to imagine that anyone in Australia printed books. He was under the impression that they were all convicts sent over from England, or people sent over from England to keep an eye on the convicts.

'So there the chimney rested, until *you*, Master Grout, pushed it on to poor Mrs Dickens's husband!'

'It was an accident, sir,' said Fabian, quietly this time.

'I think you'd better tell your story,' said Bunyon. So he did.

Life as a gypsy wasn't all brightly painted caravans, weaving baskets and wearing bright red spotty neckerchiefs. Sometimes things could get tough, wet and cold. And many people, particularly landowners, weren't always big fans of gypsies turning up on their land.

At first, Fabian's mother Hester had loved the life on the open road. Nanny Nanny Noonan had always been kind and considerate, but had brought her up to be a 'lady', and Hester Dickens was filled with a real sense of freedom and relief when she ran away with Alfie Grout (who'd come knocking at their door to sharpen scissors).

When their son, Fabian, was born, things got better and better, because the little boy loved the gypsy life and soon became a firm favourite amongst the other gypsies, who loved the way that he got up to such mischief, yet talked 'so posh-like'.

Things had got harder for Hester when her husband, Alfie, developed a permanent hacking cough. Medicine was far more primitive in Victorian times and, if you were poor, was pretty much nonexistent except for do-it-yourself herbal remedies.

This particular group of gypsies, led by Fudd, didn't include a wise old woman steeped in the old folklore of plants and their magical properties. The best anyone could suggest was that Alfie regularly eat lucky heather. This hadn't helped his year-round cough, or his indigestion, come to that, but at least it kept his breath smelling nice.

Then along came baby Oliphant. After all these years on the open road, sleeping under the stars, Hester decided that perhaps there was more to life than this, and that Oliphant, at least, should have the opportunity to lead the life that the older generation of the Dickens family had denied her.

When Hester's gypsy band found themselves in the vicinity of the Dickens family seat – no jokes, please, I mean Awful End – Hester made the decision that Oliphant should be left in the care of her uppercrust family.

She'd wrapped Oliphant in the finest blanket she could find and had written a note, enclosing one of her late father George Dickens's silk hankies, which had the Dickens family crest embroidered in one corner: a man biting his own leg. This should be proof enough that the child was one of their own.

Hester didn't tell any of the other gypsies her plan. Certainly not Chief Fudd, who would probably have forbidden it, and certainly not her husband who, despite getting more and more ill, would have insisted that they bring up their son. The only two people she told were Oliphant himself (who didn't understand a word of it, being a baby and all) and Fabian, whom she charged with taking Oliphant to Awful End.

'My instructions were to leave Ollie, with the note and hanky, where one of you would find him,' Fabian explained, 'then to stay close and watch for a few days, to make sure you treated him fairly.'

'And instead you overheard talk of beatings and saw a strange woman brandishing a stuffed ferret,' spat Fandango Jones, forgetting himself for a moment.

Even Madder Aunt Maud, who'd given the detective inspector his milk-free, sugar-free water, was now holding Malcolm again, so was able to hit the fairly well-known engineer over the head with him. (Though not hard enough to dislodge the piece of devilled kidney from his hat's brim.) 'Stoat!' she corrected him.

'But what happened to the note and your grandfather's handkerchief with the Dickens crest on it?' asked Eddie. 'It wasn't in the basket when I fished it out of the water.'

'It wasn't?' asked Fabian, in surprise.

'Do you think they'd have let a monk take him away if they'd known who he was?' asked Eddie, secretly not at all sure that, with this family, the answer would have been 'no'!

'And didn't you think it strange that we were calling the boy Ned, if we'd read your mother's communication which, no doubt, informed us that his name was Oliphant?' added Eddie's father, who'd been wheeled into the kitchen by Gibbering Jane just as Fabian had been about to explain matters.

'I . . . I didn't think,' said a crestfallen Fabian. 'So you never saw the note?'

'No,' said Eddie. 'It must have fallen from the basket into the lake before we found it.'

'But why did you put your baby brother in the

bulrushes in the first place?' asked Detective Inspector Bunyon. Being the only policeman present, he thought that it should be *he* who was asking all the questions. 'Why not leave him at the front door?'

'I didn't want to be spotted,' said Fabian. 'I wanted to leave Oliphant, then slip away to a safe distance and observe. But I didn't want it to take too long for him to be discovered, either. When I saw Eddie and her,' he nodded at EMAM, 'knocking turnips about on the lower lawn, I seized the opportunity and put Ollie within crying distance.'

'The roof,' said the detective inspector. 'How did you come to be on the roof?'

Fabian looked down at his handcuffed hands, resting in his lap. 'I soon discovered that most of the rooms in this vast place are empty and how few of you live here, so it was easy to slip in through the back door and hide myself, listening out and keeping an eye on Ollie the best I could.' He looked at Gibbering Jane. 'He obviously likes you very much,' he said. 'He doesn't coo like that for anyone but me and Mother back at camp.'

Gibbering Jane gibbered with pure pride and pleasure, like an over-excited monkey.

'It was harder to keep watch when everyone was out at the front, so looking down from the roof

160

seemed the obvious solution. The last time I was up there, I was just about to lean over the parapet when an old man dressed as a soldier appeared and gave me a terrible shock, and I accidentally pushed over this piece of stone I was leaning on.'

'Which was the chimney my mother'd left there . . . and it landed on you, Father!' said Eddie.

'I don't believe a word of it!' cried Even Madder Aunt Maud, brandishing Malcolm in the air. 'Feed him to the lions, I say!'

'No, wait,' said a familiar voice, and everyone turned to see Mr and Mrs Dickens's good friend Emily Thackery, the animal lover. Unnoticed, she'd walked into the kitchen through the back door a while since, and had been listening to the Eddie lookalike in rapt silence. 'Look at this,' she said.

Mrs Thackery spread a piece of material on the kitchen table. It was damp and looked sort of chewed, but there's no denying what it was: a handkerchief bearing the Dickens crest.

'Where did you get that?' demanded the detective inspector.

'Out of that duck with a terrible tummy ache which I took with me after my last visit,' Mrs Thackery explained. 'She's made a full recovery.'

Detective Inspector Humphrey Bunyon turned to Mr Dickens, strapped to his tea trolley. 'The decision is yours, sir,' he said. 'Do you believe the boy's story? Or do you wish me to take the matter further? Looking at him, there's not a shadow of a doubt in my mind that the lad has Dickens blood in him, and I'm inclined to believe his version of events.'

Mr Dickens smiled. 'What's a few bumps and bruises when we've just discovered a whole new branch of the family we never even knew existed? *Of course* I believe him, inspector. I consider this case closed.'

Detective Inspector Humphrey Bunyon fished a small key out of his pocket and unlocked the handcuffs, freeing Fabian's wrists. The policeman couldn't have been more delighted. He could now escape Awful End and go home and have a very large celebratory meal. 'Then my work here is at an end,' he said. 'Let me bid you all good day.' Mad Uncle Jack walked into the kitchen as the policeman walked out. 'Good day to you too, sir,' said Bunyon.

'Balderdash!' said MUJ.

★

So, as with all Eddie Dickens books before it, we come to the stage where I draw the adventure to a close and give an indication as to what happened next to those who took part.

Work soon began again on Fandango Jones's iron bridge but, halfway through the project, Mad Uncle Jack changed his mind and had him pull it down and re-use the material to build a giant something-or-other instead. I've seen pictures of the structure, and I still don't know what it was supposed to be. All I *do* know is that, during the Second World War, it was dismantled and the materials were re-used as a part of the war effort, as a result of a nationwide campaign on the home front headed by someone called Lord Beaverbrook.

There is no mention of Jones's design or work on the bridge in *Bridging the Gap: Being the Life of that Fairly Well-Known Engineer Fandango Jones.*

Detective Inspector Bunyon did manage to regain a great deal of the weight that he lost following his incarceration in a trunk at the hands of the deadly Smiley Gang (all of whom he subsequently managed to arrest, with the exception of its ringleader, Smiley Johnson). He never managed to get quite as fat as he was before. By way of compensation, though, he was promoted to Detective *Chief* Inspector not long after the events in this Further Adventure.

His desk sergeant managed to lock himself in his own handcuffs on three further occasions.

And Fabian and Baby Ollie? Why, they both came to live at Awful End, along with their parents Hester and Alfie, which is how they all come to feature in the third and final of Eddie's Further Adventures, so I won't say any more about them here.

As for the Thackerys, young David did go into the church. Many churches, in fact. And cathedrals. And rich people's houses, usually when the occupants were out or their backs were turned. As he grew older, he became more and more disenchanted with his family being so *nice* to animals and less and less keen on the idea of being a man of the cloth . . . so he became a burglar instead, specialising in stealing candle-sticks, crosses and other 'ecclesiastical furniture'. He was finally caught and, sadly, lost an eye in a prison fight before he came to trial. Apparently it was an argument over whether the correct term is 'a cake of soap' or 'a bar of soap', which was a pity, because the two are entirely different things.

Which just leaves the monks of Lamberley Monastery.

One morning, less than six weeks after the events ending on page 163 occurred, Abbot Po awoke from a dream at about three o'clock in the morning.

Dashing to the bell tower, he tolled its only bell, causing his bemused and bleary-eyed brethren to rise from their beds and assemble in the Chapter House. Once they were all present, he told them that he'd dreamt of a huge plug being pulled out of the ground and of a dreadful gurgling noise.

'I cannot tell whether it was simply something I ate or whether it was a vision,' Po said in that beautiful voice of his, 'but I cannot take the chance. I must ask you all to evacuate immediately.'

This they did and, as numerous eyewitnesses will testify, no sooner had the last man left the building – which was Po himself, of course – than there was an appalling gulping *SLERCHING* noise, and Lamberley Monastery disappeared into the ground like a sinking ship beneath the waves.

Being monks of the Bertian order, they all saw the funny side of it and were remarkably jolly about being homeless. Not that they were for long.

Where could they find a large building with enough empty rooms to offer them temporary accommodation, and at such short notice?

It was Eddie who answered the knock on the front door of Awful End later that morning. Standing on the doorstep was the ugliest man he'd ever had the privilege to know.

'Good morning Eddie,' said Po. 'Remember how we put you up for a while?'

Eddie nodded.

'I wonder if you could return the favour?'

Eddie nodded. There were monks as far as the eye could see.

THE END
until the final Further Adventure

AUTHOR'S NOTE

This is not a history book, so please don't go stating any of the information contained within it as 'fact' without checking it first. I've always found *Old Roxbee's* books an excellent source of information but, then again, that could be another of my lies.

The Philip Ardagh Club

COLLECT some fantastic **Philip Ardagh** merchandise.

WHAT **YOU** HAVE TO DO:

You'll find numbered tokens to collect in all Philip Ardagh's fiction books published after 01/04/05. There are 2 tokens in each hardback and 1 token in each paperback. Cut them out and send them to us complete with the form below (or a photocopy of the form) and you'll get these great gifts:

> **2 tokens** = a Philip Ardagh poster
> **3 tokens** = a Philip Ardagh mousemat
> **4 tokens** = a Philip Ardagh pencil case and stationery set

Please send the form, together with your tokens or photocopies of them, to:

Philip Ardagh promotion, Faber and Faber Ltd, 3 Queen Square, London, WC1N 3AU.

Please ensure that each token has a different number.

1. This offer can not be used in conjunction with any other offer and is non transferable. 2. No cash alternative is offered. 3. If under 18 please get permission and help from a parent or guardian to enter. 4. Please allow at least 28 days delivery. 5. No responsibility can be taken for items lost in the post. 6. This offer will close on 31/04/07. 7. Offer open to readers in the UK and Ireland ONLY.

Name: ....
Address: ....
....
....
Town: ....
Postcode: ....
Age & Date of Birth: ....
Girl or boy: ....

Philip Ardagh Club
token number 8

Philip Ardagh Club
token number 9

For more infomation and competitions join the Philip Ardagh Club on-line.
Visit www.philipardagh.com